Death of an Old Goat

'Isn't it *dreadful*,' said Lucy Wickham with ghoulish pleasure into the telephone. 'I haven't got any of the details yet, but as far as I can make out his throat was cut.'

'Poor old chappie,' said Mrs Turberville at the other end. 'Seemed so full of life yesterday, too.'

It was the first time for many decades that Professor Belville-Smith had been described as full of life, and he was not alive to appreciate it . . .

Also in Mysterious Press by Robert Barnard

**UNRULY SON
DEATH ON THE HIGH Cs**

DEATH OF AN OLD GOAT

OLD GOAT

Robert Barnard

ARROW BOOKS

For Louise

Mysterious Press books (UK) are published
in association with Arrow Books Limited
20 Vauxhall Bridge Road, London SW1U 25A

An imprint of Random Century Group

London Melbourne Sydney Auckland
Johannesburg and agencies throughout the world

First published by William Collins Sons & Co. Ltd. 1974

Mysterious Press edition 1990

© Robert Barnard 1974

Set in Sabon
by JH Graphics Ltd, Reading

Made and printed in Great Britain
Courier International, Tiptree, Essex

ISBN 0 09 958270 8

CONTENTS

CHAPTER ONE

At Drummondale Station

In the late autumn sunshine the little station at Drummondale dozed on, regardless of its vital position in the nationwide network of connecting lines which the State Railways Board mentioned in its advertisements, and regardless too of the fact that the express train from Sydney was due in two minutes' time. For the fact that a train was due rarely implied that it was about to arrive. And if it did turn up, by some quirk of organizational chance, the station could put itself into its usual state of preparedness by the ticket-collector lounging out on to the platform from the station-master's office (where at this very moment he was admiring himself in front of a long, dirty mirror, his oily hands twisted round behind his back, poised to squeeze a festering yellow boil on his neck) and by the stray porter, who was forbidden by his doctor from carrying anything, pushing his cap back a fraction of an inch from its present position, where it was shielding most of his face from the early evening sun. But as yet there was no sign of either functionary stirring himself into what passed for action, so it was clear that a train was expected only in the most nominal sense.

Professor Wickham walked in his tense, abrupt way up and down the station, sometimes banging one fist nervously into the palm of the other hand, sometimes grinning automatically – in the way he did to students that he thought he might have seen before – at a couple of stray dogs running along the platform and across the line. His hair was very fair, and brushed forwards, and his eyes were an indeterminate blue. From a distance he looked like a dreamy Scandinavian; from close to he looked merely ineffectual. He was medium-height, but thick-set, and his hair flopped over his eyes periodically, making him look much younger than he really was. When he had been appointed to his chair at Drummondale he had been young to be a Professor, though not as young to be a Professor as most Australian Professors are. Now, twelve years later, and after several disappointed attempts to be called to Chairs elsewhere, he was beginning to lose his pleasant, puppyish air, and to settle despondently into his fifties, conscious that here he was, and here he was likely to stay. At the moment he looked, and was, distinctly worried, and when a glance at his watch coincided in his perambulations with the door of the station-master's office, he put his head inside, and met the suspicious gaze of the youthful ticket-collector, who was wiping pus from his neck with a dirty rag.

Professor Wickham cleared his throat nervously:

'Er . . . er . . . could you tell me when the train from Sydney is due?' he asked, in that tentative tone of voice he used for members of the lower orders he thought might turn nasty. The young man looked at him aggressively, and sized him up as a University bloke. Not one of the local graziers, and not likely to complain.

'Do you know this is private, this room?'

'Er – private?'

'Yes, private. You see that notice on the door? Private, it says. P-R-I- – can you see it?'

'Oh, er, yes . . . yes.'

'Well, then. Private, see. The general public not allowed in. Get it?'

'Yes, oh yes, sorry,' said Professor Wickham, withdrawing his head.

Having won his little victory, the ticket-collector decided to be obliging, in the best traditions of his service. He lounged over to the door, and draped himself by the door-post.

'Now, what was it?'

'Er – is the train from Sydney due?' said Wickham.

'Oh, it's due,' said the young man.

'And when will it arrive then?'

'I don't know, do I? Your guess is as good as mine, I'd say – probably better, in fact, 'cos I'm not guessing.'

He turned his eyes towards the horizon, in the direction of Brisbane, to signify his professional indifference to whatever might be coming his way from Sydney. Professor Wickham resumed his lonely stroll, thinking wistfully of the polite employees of the British Railway system in his Oxford days, whom his memory had covered with a sentimental haze. He had not been married when he first went to England, and almost everything that had happened to him before his marriage was covered in his mind with a sentimental haze. There had been precious little room for sentiment since.

It really was very difficult. Lucy had impressed on him not to be late, because they had to be over at the Turbervilles' by half past eight, and it was a forty-mile drive. In the ordinary course of events Lucy was far from unappreciative of a visiting Professor as a means of relieving the rural monotony of the University of Drummondale – and she particularly appreciated a specimen from one of the older Universities. But it was especially unfortunate that the present one, with all the glories of Oxbridge on his head, had happened to coincide with the twenty-first party of the eldest

Turberville, a party she had gone to enormous lengths to get an invitation to. The Professor would have to be shunted off to his motel for the night in plenty of time for Wickham to get back home, dress, and drive himself and Lucy out to the barbecue-dance. That was how Lucy had planned it. And if the State Railways didn't fit in with her plans, all hell would break loose over the head of her husband − which was not logical, even if it was standard marital practice.

Professor Wickham wondered a little to himself about the arrangements. Something always seemed to go wrong when Visiting Professors arrived. There was that vulgar little Welshman whom they'd taken out to the McKays the night he arrived to see what real graziers' hospitality was like. The only glimpse the students had caught of him was his rigid form being dumped on to the train, en route from one cancelled lecture in Drum-mondale to another cancelled lecture in Brisbane. Then there was the swinging American Professor whom Lucy had refused to have in the house, and whom he'd had put up in the guest-room of one of the two women's colleges. He blamed himself a good deal for that. Of course there was no guarantee it had been his child. Daisy Bates College prided itself on the nunnery-like strictness of its rules, but Australia was an open-air country, and what couldn't be done in the comfort of a bed could very easily take place in the snake-infested undergrowths around the campus. Still, the girl had said it was the American and it didn't do the Department any good.

He ran over things as presently arranged. He might be able to pass off tonight, since it could be presented as the tactful thing to leave Professor Belville-Smith to have a good night's rest after his tiring journey. He was as old as the hills, of course − otherwise he wouldn't be out here at all. It was really incredible how old all the visiting lecturers sent by institutions like the British

Council were. Perhaps the more vigorous younger scholars insisted on Europe or America, and the ones who were too old to have any 'pull' were given Australia. It hardly improved the British image. But if the old chap was just dying to collapse into his bed that was all to the good. Professor Wickham did wonder about arrangements for the next few days, though. He had sensed an undercurrent of resentment among his own staff over the tea-and-scones arrangement for tomorrow afternoon. Yet Lucy had been very insistent that this was all she was going to give the 'academics'. Could it have got to their ears that there was going to be a party the very same evening for Belville-Smith to which only the local notables were to be invited? Wickham sighed. Of course it must have reached them. Nothing was secret in a town the size of Drummondale. That must explain their coldness to him. That dreadful girl Alice O'Brien had practically cut him in the corridor that morning! Cut by a temporary lecturer! Well, her time would be up soon. Perhaps he could get some nice young Englishman to take her place. Lucy always liked the ones fresh from Oxbridge, and they were always polite to her for the first year or so. It made things so much easier. And he did think they gave the department *tone*. Most of the other departments were desperately lacking in *tone*.

He sighed, and looked into the darkness. There was no sign of the train. Lucy would be livid with him. Why had she never got livid with him before they were married? It would have made things so much easier. He would certainly still have married her, but there would be less of this feeling of having been *had*.

As the pace of the Sydney-Brisbane express train slowed down to a near halt going up the Northern ranges, the cold of an Australian autumn on the Northern Tableland struck chill into the aged bones of Professor

11

Belville-Smith. He sat huddled in the corner of a dull and dirty first-class compartment, which had not been thoroughly cleaned since the last Royal Tour, and which he was sharing with various less than first-class companions. At the beginning of the day, which seemed an age away, his mind had just been lively enough to take notice of these companions, to tut-tut mentally at their vowel-sounds and their shirts, and even to throw glances of conspiratorial horror at the British Council representative who had seen him off in Sydney; but the long day's journey into night across the grey-green monotony of the Australian countryside had dampened his far-from-sparkling spirits, so that now, when very little was to be seen outside, he was close to extinction.

As he looked out into the murk at the grazing sheep, and they looked at him with an equally lively interest, the rhythm of the wheels made words in his brain, and the words made fragments of the lectures, the lectures he had been giving to large and small groups of bored students and teachers in the lecture-rooms of Universities, in capital city after hideous capital city. 'The CHARM of her PROSE and the GRACE of her MANNER.' The words were familiar to him not only from their recent over-repetition: they also seemed, now, a part of his boyhood. He had been delivering that lecture since 1922. The same lecture, in the same words. Less frequently of late, perhaps. For by the time he got to Mrs Gaskell the students had sometimes faded away to nothingness, and he had packed his lecture away again and slowly made his way back to his college, for he was not one of those who believed that a lecture should be given, regardless of whether or not there were students there to hear it. That was carrying things a little too far. Last term he had not even gone along to see if there was any audience for some of his later lectures – 'Charles Reade, an unjustly neglected novelist' and 'Mrs Oliphant – a lesser Trollope'. Perhaps it was better that

12

the latter lecture never got delivered these days. How strange that the revival in Mrs Oliphant's reputation which he had been predicting all these years had never actually come about! Why, he wondered? It must be something to do with the modern world. But he turned his old mind from that thought with horror. The modern world was something he had never seen, and didn't want to see. He had a vague idea that, if he didn't take any notice of it, it might pass away before very long, and his own world come back.

The rhythm of the wheels changed: 'PUNgent she CAN be; CRUel she NEVER is.' His eyes watered a little. Dear Jane Austen! Looking around the other occupants of the compartment he comforted himself with the thought that they never, never in a million years, would appreciate Jane Austen. She was his Jane! A combination of Mrs Gaskell and Virginia Woolf, with very little of the real Jane. He had got a good deal of quiet enjoyment out of giving that lecture to those vulgar-shirted yokels in those disgustingly dirty cities he had just come from. He felt an emissary from a forgotten world, bringing a fragrant lost culture to the raw, raucous civilization which now and then had forced itself on his notice in the last few weeks, but had mostly drifted past his old eyes, unattended. Perhaps he had planted some seeds. . . ?

A welcome feeling in his stomach told him that he was hungry, and then his brain, slowly reacting, told him that he was in Australia. An acute pang of disappointment made him pout out his lower lip like a baby. His hunger was unlikely to be satisfactorily appeased. To cover his gastronomical experiences of the last few months he had come up with a formula of 'quantity rather than quality' – not an original observation, but one he was rather proud of. Because it didn't apply only to food, though he applied it mainly to food, because food was what he thought of for much of the time. He peered out at the endless, dusty landscape. Quantity rather than quality.

Suddenly there were two or three houses together, and then more, in a sort of improvised road. They were coming to a little town. He looked closer. Surely this could not be a University town. No. Obviously just another of those little country places they had been passing all day.

The train pulled into a station, and the placard along the platform, hardly legible for the accumulated dust of this throat-clogging country read DRUMMONDALE. The name range a vague bell in the back of his mind. Oh dear. He must have arrived.

It struck Professor Belville-Smith, or rather it edged its way into his consciousness, that the little man who had met him was distinctly in a hurry. The handshake had been twice up and down, and he had been hurried through the ticket-barrier as fast as the ticket-collector, whose hand seemed deftly able to grasp any ticket but his, would allow. Now he was being hustled into a dusty Ford Cortina as if he were a troublesome old nanny on a family outing, and he was not at all sure that he liked it. Of course the car refused to obey the driver in a hurry. This was no doubt partly due to the fact that he did not put the clutch in before trying to start it. They drove off jerkily into the monotonous streets, with the shabby wooden houses and the tired grass and hedges, like every suburb he had seen in this old young country, only tireder and shabbier. Professor Belville-Smith tried to formulate a description of it all. 'Like a recent settlement in Purgatory,' he said to himself. He smiled: that was really rather good. Should he suggest it to the funny little man beside him? Perhaps not. He had noticed in Australians a certain touchiness about their own country. Certain remarks he had made, intended to be only obliquely insulting, had met with disconcertingly violent retorts. It didn't do to tempt Providence when you were hungry.

'You must be very tired,' said Professor Wickham.

'Just a little, just a little,' said the Distinguished Guest, feeling much refreshed by his phrase-making.

'We must have a chat about your work on the Augustans, when you're feeling less tired,' said Professor Wickham.

The Distinguished Guest racked his brains to remember what work he might once have done on the Augustans. Of course – the pamphlet on the lyrical poetry of John Gay, the product of an unusual outburst of energy in early middle-age. How strange that anyone should still be reading that.

'Delighted,' he murmured urbanely.

'Not now of course,' said his host. 'It is *such* a tiring journey.'

'But *most* interesting,' lied Belville-Smith, gallantly, with an unpleasant feeling that he was in the way, and would shortly be disposed of.

'I always fly myself,' said Wickham, changing gear with a horror-film shriek. 'Less tiring.'

Through the deepening darkness they hastened erratically. A short stretch of neon-lighting suggested that they might be in the main street, and a few drunks rolled across the headlights of Professor Wickham's car. But they turned off, and almost immediately approached the illuminated signs of the Yarumba Motel which lit up rows of garishly painted little chalets. Professor Wickham stopped abruptly outside the reception hut, and jumped out. Belville-Smith looked around him with growing distaste. It was *exactly* the same as every other motel he had stayed at in this straggling, beastly country – just a bit smaller, perhaps, but basically exactly the same. He might be in Perth, or Adelaide, or Melbourne, or Sydney, or Newcastle. Or a recent settlement in Purgatory, he said to himself, with a self-satisfied smile.

'You'll be very comfortable here,' said Professor Wickham, emerging brusquely from reception. 'Motels are the only places to stay, here in Australia, you know.'

'So it seems,' said Professor Belville-Smith.

He felt himself speedily decanted from the car and hustled into his predictable room.

'There's everything here,' said Professor Wickham, glancing around quickly. The room was furnished by the same computer which had furnished the motels in Perth, Adelaide, Melbourne, Sydney and Newcastle. 'Shower, bath, sofa, table, desk, you see.' He was very clearly making for the door.

'Food,' said Professor Belville-Smith.

'I beg your pardon,' said Wickham, caught in mid-escape.

'Food. I have not yet eaten my evening meal.'

'Oh! Well, you just ring. Ring the reception, and give your order. They'll serve it in here.'

Professor Belville-Smith advanced purposefully on the telephone. Wickham made good his escape while he could.

'I'll pick you up at nine tomorrow.'

'Do they serve evening meals at the Yarumba?' said Wickham to Lucy, as they drove out to the barbecue-dance.

'Of course they don't,' said Lucy, dabbing at her layers of make-up in the driving mirror. 'Get a move on, you idiot. You've wasted enough time on that old fool as it is.'

CHAPTER TWO

At Beecher's

Professor Belville-Smith perched his tired body irritably on the side of the bed, blinked twice, and picked up the telephone. Really, the man was most inconsiderate – most inconsiderate. Why, he'd hardly even bothered to disguise his intention of dumping his guest, of forcing him to spend a lonely evening in a hideous motel in a one-horse town . . . It was all very well to keep saying 'You must be tired'; it had never once occurred to him to say 'You must be hungry'. It was, in Professor Belville-Smith's opinion, a much more pertinent observation. He had found that, as he grew older, he needed less sleep than formerly, perhaps because he spent so much of the day only half-awake. He had *not* found that he needed less food. Quite the contrary. And he could not eat just anything. The meal served on the train had been too disgusting for words. He was conscious, now, of being very hungry indeed. He banged resentfully on the receiver-rest of the motel telephone.

'Yes, can I help you, sir?' came a voice of killing Australian gentility.

'Yes, you can. I wish to order dinner,' said Belville-Smith, in the voice he used for negligent servants.

'I beg your pardon?'

'I . . . wish . . . to . . . order . . . dinner,' he said, spacing out his words as if they were milestones.

'I'm afraid, sir, you're labouring under a misap-prehension. Dinner we *don't* serve.' The implication was that any other meal he might care to name was well within their capacity.

'What? You don't serve dinner?'

'No, sir. But if you would care to order your breakfast for tomorrow you will find an order form . . .'

'I don't want breakfast,' he almost screamed into the telephone. 'I'm hungry now. I want my dinner.'

He heard, though clearly he wasn't meant to, a muttered 'They're just like little children, at times.' Then the voice, resuming its Kensington vowel-sounds, came through loud and clear again.

'You could try Beecher's Hotel, you know. Just down the road and turn to the right. Or there's a very nice little Chinese caf*fay* . . .'

'Chinese! Do you think I'm going to eat that rubbish?' shouted Belville-Smith, breathlessly.

'I couldn't say, I'm sure,' said the voice coolly. 'But we must try not to be prejudiced, mustn't we?'

He found himself sharply and pointedly cut off. He sat down on his bed again, the whimpers rising uncon-trollably from his empty stomach. Nowhere else had he been treated like this. If you're an Oxford Professor and consent to come to the back of beyond, you do at least expect to be an honoured guest. You don't expect to be stranded, deserted, left to starve. His mind ran lovingly over the things he would say to Professor Wickham tomorrow, then tore itself reluctantly away. When you are old, you have to concentrate on one thing at a time. He concentrated unremittingly on food. Buttoning his coat around him again, he aimed himself at the door.

Irritation giving purpose to his steps, he made his way through the courtyard of the motel, through the sounds of love-making and television commercials, and turned towards what he thought must be the centre of the town. The night air woke him up a little and he looked curiously round him. All those square, verandahed houses with their paint peeling off and their drab and dry little gardens. Truly, he was in limbo, he thought to himself. He set off towards the sound of cars and juke-boxes. The centre of the town, he soon discovered, was a street, a short street, intersected, always at right angles, by other streets. Australia, he thought, was a country of circles and squares, and they could plan their towns in no other way. One was intolerably confusing, the other simply boring. Where was this hotel? He peered dimly up the street. It reminded him of what the Wild West of America must have been like in the days of his youth: taverns with long balconies all round them, and posts to tie the horses to. Some of the men were not unlike characters he had once seen in a Wild West film long ago, in the days before films began to talk. If those things with balconies really were taverns, then presumably one of them was his destination. He didn't fancy walking into one; in fact, he rather thought he might get shot at. But he forgot his skin in his concern for his stomach, and he walked along the street peering hungrily about him.

The smell that first assailed his nostrils was of beer rather than food, and the garish advertisements placarded along the wall were of beer too – sun-lit, bubbling glasses, a mere crude appealing to the thirsty. But looking at the sign over the door he realized thankfully that he had reached his destination. As he walked up the steps of Beecher's Hotel and into the foyer – decorated with an enormous bunch of gladioli – the door to the saloon bar was pushed open, and an intolerable stench of beer and beer and beer flooded in his direction. For a moment the potency of it nearly made him lose his balance, then, gasping, choking, he stumbled faster than he had done for thirty years up the remaining stairs, until he reached the comparative odourlessness of the reception-desk.

'The dining-room,' he choked hoarsely.

The young man behind the desk surveyed him for a few moments, then jerked his thumb lazily to his left. It was impertinence, but this was not the moment to protest. Professor Belville-Smith turned and tottered towards the sanctum of the dining-room; pushing open the swinging glass doors, he sank gratefully into the first chair that offered.

It took him some minutes to get his breath back. He mopped his forehead with his handkerchief, and cleaned his spectacles meticulously. As he puffed and tut-tutted himself back to normality some impressions of the place gradually filtered through to him. Colours – off-white (table-cloths) and dirty blue (walls). The place seemed to be empty – ah, no; not quite. There were two young people at the table next to his own. Otherwise the place was entirely untenanted. At any rate there wouldn't be any difficulty in getting service here. His eye ranged down the dreary length of the room. By the door at the far end he thought he could make out the figure of what must be the waitress. She was sitting on a table, apparently cleaning her nails with one of the table-knives, and swapping insults with somebody behind the far door. That, he presumed, must be the kitchen.

He collected his thoughts and signed to her. As if her eyes were unable to penetrate the immense distance she ignored him, and went on cleaning her nails and shouting. He waited, and signed again. She rapped out a little tune with the knife on the table, shouted a last cheerful insult at her antagonist on the other side of the door, and then slowly made the long trek over to him. She turned out to be a rather cheery slattern, with a stained apron and greasy hair.

'Me feet are killing me today,' she said genially. 'Something yer'd like?'

'I would like the menu, please,' said Belville-Smith, distinctly, as if he were talking to an idiot. As, indeed, he was sure he was. She looked at him doubtfully.

'We've got a lovely bit of steak,' she said encouragingly. 'Wouldn't that suit yer?'

'The menu.'

'And the fish is nice. Real lovely it smells out there. I'd pick yer a real good bit.'

'What *kind* of fish?' said Belville-Smith, pettishly.

'There yer've got me,' said the waitress.

'I want the menu,' he said, raising his quavering voice in a discontented plainsong.

'Oh well, no peace for the wicked,' said the waitress, and ambled off to the distant table whence she had come, and returned with a fly-blown, gravy-stained, red-wine-glass-ringed menu of greater antiquity than most things Professor Belville-Smith had seen in this plastic-coated country. It was a mis-typed list of five or six dishes of predictable awfulness. Clipped to the side was a slip which read: 'Chef's special for today: mince curry.' Belville-Smith gazed at it, sunk in dreadful gloom, while the waitress perched her broad bottom on the edge of his table.

He was startled out of his depression by a voice from the next table – an English voice:

'Can we help you?'

It was a rather spotty and extremely ill-dressed young man, who was sitting with his back to him, but had now swivelled round to address him. His companion was a woman – sharp-eyed behind her thick glasses, with a long string of coloured beads round her neck and her make-up badly applied to her sunburnt skin.

'We thought you mightn't be used to the hotels in Australia,' said the young man. Professor Belville-Smith even realized that his accent was educated English. How did educated Englishmen land up in a place like this? 'In fact,' the voice went on, 'we wondered whether you mightn't be our visiting Professor.'

Professor Belville-Smith, who had not mixed with the general public for many years, was not used to the

21

striking-up of instant acquaintanceships. At any other time he would have administered a peppery snub. However, he felt himself to be decidedly in a storm, and he thought that the rather unprepossessing young man might represent any port. He therefore decided to advance half-way to meet him.

'Well, I don't know, just possibly . . . I *am* visiting here, but . . . what college . . . er, what *department*?'

'English.'

'Ah yes, well that is my . . . er . . . my *subject*.'

'So we were right, then. You must be Professor Belville-Smith.'

'Er, yes. We haven't been introduced, but . . .'

'No. I suppose Professor Wickham is neglecting you as usual, is he?'

The words struck a very real responsive chord.

'*Yes*. Yes, he *is*.'

'Thought so. You're not the first, you know. Look, would you care to join us?'

'Yes, I will.' And he gathered up his ill-co-ordinated body, and moved it to the next table. If his stomach was not to be well fed, he could at least give some vent to his grievance. 'Yes, he *is*. I've never been so neglected in my life.'

'Professor Belville-Smith will have T-bone steak,' said the spotty youth to the waitress. 'And bring another bottle of Diwarra claret.'

'Right-ee-ho,' said the waitress, apparently glad to see her little flock happy.

'Diwarra claret,' said Professor Belville-Smith faintly.

'It'll go down,' said the woman sitting opposite him.

'The T-bone is the only thing worth eating,' said the boy. 'You really shouldn't have come here.'

'Except there's nowhere else,' said the girl, whose voice was rich in strangulated Australian dipthongs.

Professor Belville-Smith was finding their conversation a source of bewilderment to him.

'Er . . . you are –' he paused, as a thought struck him – 'not *students*.' He looked at them out of his watery eyes. 'I hope I have not been at all indiscreet.'

'Relax,' said the woman.

'We're lecturers in Wickham's department,' said the boy. 'I'm Bill Bascomb and this is Alice O'Brien.'

Professor Belville-Smith sank back in relief. Of course the woman was a lecturer. He should have seen that. He'd come to know this type from Perth to Sydney. Whereas the women academics at Oxford had usually resigned themselves long ago to their lack of feminity, here they made efforts to be both academic and normal, an impossible combination. But the boy . . . he couldn't place the boy.

'I'm just out from England,' Bill Bascomb explained. 'Only got here a couple of months ago.'

'Oxford perhaps?' murmured Professor Belville-Smith.

'Balliol,' said the boy.

'Ah yes,' said the distinguished guest. 'I don't very often run across the young men from Balliol.'

'Do we have to hush our voices every time we mention the old college?' said Alice O'Brien, in an irritated voice.

'Get lost,' said Bill Bascomb.

'We thought Bobby would get rid of you as soon as decent tonight,' said Alice O'Brien, turning to Professor Belville-Smith.

'Or even earlier,' said Bill Bascomb.

'Party at the Turbervilles' tonight,' said Alice. 'Son's got a coming-of-age. Officially, that is. Mental age of ten, but nobody seems to notice.'

'Marvellous what money will do,' said Bill.

'Five cars,' said Alice. 'And they use the Volksie as a hen-run.'

Professor Belville-Smith felt that his bewilderment was not being lessened. He almost welcomed the return of the waitress, still intolerably cheery. She placed a dark bottle between her sturdy knees, and extracted the cork. She wiped around the rim with a greasy cloth, and slopped out a glassful. Then she looked into the particled depths of the glass.

'Cork,' she said, grinning cheekily at Professor Belville-Smith. 'How's that affect yer?'

'Badly,' said Alice. 'Get another glass.'

Professor Belville-Smith looked uncertain whether to burst into smoke or tears.

'I really don't understand,' he said loudly, as a new glass of quite drinkable red wine was put in front of him. He sipped it fretfully. 'I really don't. Everywhere else . . . *everywhere* . . . people take care of me. I'm honoured. The honoured guest. And then I come here, to this dreadful place, and . . . and . . .'

He was conscious of two pairs of eyes looking at him. Was it sympathy or amusement in their eyes?

'We *are* sorry,' said Bill.

'But what can you expect from Bobby?' asked Alice.

'It's not so much him as his wife. It's Lucy that puts him up to most of these things he does.'

'You'll meet her,' said Alice. 'She'll be all over you tomorrow. But today was the Turberville party. And she's been working for an invitation for weeks.'

'I shall protest tomorrow,' said Professor Belville-Smith, grabbing his napkin eagerly as a plate was put in front of him.

'You do that small thing,' said Alice, obviously pleased. She and Bill Bascomb, their own plates empty, sat and watched with fatherly interest as the visiting Professor tucked into the steak with something between a hearty appetite and naked greed. The steak was tender but over-cooked, though Belville-Smith was much too hungry to complain. In any case he had got used to the Australian habit of being proud of half-way perfection. The steak went down not unpleasantly, and the wine sent little fingers of warmth exploring through his body;

his stomach regained its natural equilibrium, and he mellowed towards the two young people who had taken him under their wing; they were raw of course, but then he found that all young people were raw these days. And, as junior followers of his own calling, he felt they were entitled to any scraps of graciousness he could find the strength to throw their way.

'I shall look forward greatly to meeting you again tomorrow,' he said expansively. He picked up the glass of brandy, which they had suggested he should take without coffee. ('even more disgusting than English coffee' Bascomb had said). He toyed with it a little apprehensively; his drinking experiences had been so variable in this country.

'We're looking forward to your lectures,' said Alice, lying.

'I enjoyed your Victorian series so much at Oxford,' said Bill Bascomb, lying.

Professor Belville-Smith positively bloomed. It did not occur to him that if Bascomb had been to his lectures he ought to have identified him more confidently. He was past the stage where he investigated compliments to ascertain how sincere they were. The mere fact of receiving them was enough, and was becoming rarer. He smiled with gratified vanity.

'Ah, did you? Good . . . good. One should not say so, of course, but there are one or two touches in those lectures which I must admit I myself do not . . . er . . . despise.'

'The one on Mrs Gaskell I remember particularly,' said Bill (who had in fact once read an article by Belville-Smith entitled 'Thackeray, ambivalent jester', and had avoided his lectures entirely, deciding that he could not bear to hear all the great Victorians being reduced to the level of a Fanny Burney).

'Ah yes. Such a difficult subject for . . . er . . . modern youth. So dependent, you see, on an *atmosphere*, on nuances. Yes, I'm glad you liked that one. I have been interested to see how that goes down with . . . er . . . Australians.'

'Talking of Cranford,' said Alice, 'we meet for tea and buns at the Wickhams' tomorrow.'

'Oh dear, tea and buns . . .'

'Tea and buns at four for the Department, then a party later for the gentry,' said Bill Bascomb. 'Would you believe it? That's typical of the Wickhams.'

'You mean they will be expecting me to go to both?' said Professor Belville-Smith.

'Oh yes,' they said in chorus.

'I will not. It's quite preposterous to arrange such a programme without consulting me.'

'It is,' said the chorus.

'An unheard-of liberty. I shall refuse.'

'You tell him tomorrow,' said Alice, with barely concealed glee.

'I shall. One party at most. And I shall expect to meet the Department there. It is the least he can do.'

'You've no idea how least Bobby can do if he tries,' said Alice. The two young lecturers were enjoying themselves, and scenting free alcohol from their Professor, a rare experience.

'I shall insist,' said Belville-Smith, struggling to his feet, 'and I shall look forward to seeing you again.'

'Do you know your way back?' asked Bill.

'Well . . . I'm . . . not sure . . . If you could *direct* me . . .' It was a blatant appeal for help.

'Let's settle up,' said Bill, 'and we'll see you home.'

So when the waitress had reluctantly counted out their change from a dirty purse apparently secreted among her underclothes, they took him back to his motel, past the spewing drunks at the entrance to Beecher's, and along the dark, inhospitable side-streets, walking at a suitably gentle pace. They left him in his

26

room, and drove back to their respective colleges, eminently pleased with their night's work.

'Don't get in early tomorrow,' said Alice to Bill as they parted by their cars. 'Bobby will be needing cigarettes the whole morning.'

Professor Belville-Smith lay on his bed, trying to solace his still rumbling discontent with a few pages of *Cousin Phyllis*. Never had he felt so strongly the need of a little old-world charm.

CHAPTER THREE

Guest Lecture

The next morning proved a trying one for Professor Wickham, as Alice O'Brien had foreseen. Though he did not, strictly speaking, have a hangover, he did have that heavy, dehydrated feeling which comes from rather too much alcohol and decidedly too little sleep. He was certainly in no mood to cope with querulous visiting Professors, whose grievances had grown with being slept on. Professor Belville-Smith was not accustomed to hiding his discontents – his own Senior Common-Room feared them greatly – and his grievances had been augmented by the experience of breakfast, which had become indeed, an almost daily grievance during his stay in Australia.

'I was offered steak and eggs, steak, bacon and eggs, steak, bacon and kidney, mutton chop, kidney and eggs and I don't know what,' he said. 'And though I ordered bacon and eggs, it came with a mutton chop. Never have I seen anything so greasy and disgusting in my life. Is all the cooking out here done by *blacks*?'

'Well, that could be, yes,' said Professor Wickham, bustling him out to the car.

'I begin to wonder whether I should have come here at all,' said the guest, as they started up in the familiar kangaroo fashion.

28

Here Professor Wickham made the tactical error of trying to make his guest feel more wanted. He mentioned the projected tea-party, and the more select gathering arranged for later. He did it in the manner of a foolish mother promising a child two birthday parties.

'I'm afraid I must decline,' said Professor Belville-Smith, tetchily. 'Two such occasions on one day are more than I can take. You must remember that I am an old man. I have had to face a extraordinary schedule in this . . . country. An evening party perhaps, which I can leave early if I feel tired, but both, no.'

Professor Wickham oozed geniality. This suited him fine, and Lucy would be pleased. It would cost him no embarrassment to cancel the tea-party for his members of staff. He was so used to slighting them and offending their feelings that he was hardened by usage as strongly as the Act V Macbeth. Whatever point was there in being Professor if one had to kow-tow to one's staff all the time?

'That's quite all right,' he said. 'We'll just have the evening party. No trouble at all to call off the other.'

'I shall look forward to meeting the members of your staff in the evening then,' said Belville-Smith, partly out of senile malice, partly out of a genuine sense of his obligations to the two young people of the night before.

Professor Wickham's heart sank. Whatever was Lucy going to say? If there was anything she hated it was wasting good alcohol on University people below the rank of Professor. As he drove through the depressing flat landscape towards the University he got a distinct impression that the old man by his side was hugging himself with pleasure – as if he felt he had got his revenge. He rather fancied that if arrangements for today went off no better than those for yesterday, the distinguished guest would be telling a long story about his defective hospitality to his opposite number in Brisbane before very long. Not that the opposite number would be surprised.

The University was situated three or four miles out of the city of Drummondale: the city fathers had insisted on this, for they feared contamination. The first one saw of it was a series of blocks and huts at the bottom of a hill, which Professor Wickham pointed out by name as some of the colleges into which the university was divided. Up the hill were toiling strings of students in jeans and odd green gowns, and at the top of the hill there were more blocks and huts, which were apparently the departments, and a large Edwardian gentleman's residence which sprouted and straggled in all directions, and had caused John Betjeman to chortle appreciatively. This was the nucleus of the university, and now housed the administration who not unnaturally kept the best thing for themselves. Professor Wickham flapped his hands at all these objects of interest, and Professor Belville-Smith turned his head in their direction, and practised non-seeing.

When they arrived at the English Department, which was housed in temporary accommodation of a depressing permanence, the first sound that met their ears was that of Alice O'Brien, swapping words along the length of the corridor with a colleague in her most calling-the-cattle-home voice. Professor Wickham assumed his obligatory shudder, and was just wondering whether he could avoid introducing Professor Belville-Smith to the home-grown phenomenon when she emerged to view and hailed their visitor like a long-lost friend. The voice which affected Wickham like a blatant threat seemed to have no terrors for Belville-Smith, who gravely and courteously shook her hand. Professor Wickham gathered that they had met the previous evening, and wondered apprehensively what the topic of conversation had been. He'd never liked that bitch, and neither

30

had Lucy. Much better to stick to raw Englishmen: they might be incompetent, but at least they had a modicum of style. What a damned shame O'Brien was so competent; no chance of terminating her engagement prematurely on that score. Still, at least her temporary status made her the natural for loading all the unpleasant jobs off on to.

'Perhaps you would show Professor Belville-Smith around until it's time for his lecture, Miss O'Brien?' he said hurriedly, and bustled into his room to phone Lucy.

Alice looked at the distinguished guest, who still retained some of his early-morning spryness.

'Do you really want to go and view this collection of old sheds?' she asked.

'No,' said Professor Belville-Smith.

'You'll see enough of them in an hour's time,' said Alice; 'you're lecturing in one.'

She suddenly held up a finger, and they were both silent. From Professor Wickham's room came the plaintive tones peculiar to men with unreasonable wives:

'I know, dear, I know . . . Yes, I know . . . I KNOW . . . But what can I do? He forced my hand . . . Yes, I know . . . But he won't come at all if we *don't* invite them . . . Yes, he *is* capable of doing that . . . Yes, he is old, but he's tough . . . They'll have to come in the evening . . . We can see they don't get too much.'

Alice turned to Professor Belville-Smith, with a broad smile of congratulation.

'Good on you,' she said. 'Why don't we go along to my room?'

Professor Belville-Smith looked curiously round Alice O'Brien's study to see what an Australian academic's room was like. On one shelf of the book-case was Campbell's *Anglo-Saxon Grammar*, a Middle-English dictionary, and an Agatha Christie. Just above these was a large flagon of dry sherry, three-quarters empty, a bottle of whisky, a bottle of gin, a bottle of brandy, a bottle of curaçao, two flagons of cheap red and white wine, and a large collection of tonic water, bitter lemon, ginger ale and a soda siphon.

'Have a drink,' said Alice.

'At this time of day?' said Professor Belville-Smith.

'Religious scruples?' asked Alice.

'I'll have a whisky.'

Professor Belville-Smith eased himself into the only comfortable chair, and the hour passed rather pleasantly in a swapping of derogatory opinions about a wide range of Australian academics who had been Professor Belville-Smith's hosts over the last few weeks. Professor Belville-Smith had a vein of cattiness which had not been very extensively mined of late, perhaps because his growing detachment from the life around him meant that most of the people he wanted to be catty about were dead, or as good as. Thus, though none of his hosts had been as negligent as Professor Wickham, he found it in him to say something delicately nasty about every one of them, and Alice stored up his remarks to report back to her friends in the various capitals.

The distinguished guest was just beginning to feel warm and rather mellow, floating happily back to the mood of sluggish malice in which he existed at Oxford, when Professor Wickham came to get them, and they all scrambled into their gowns. In the corridor the Department was gathering dutifully to troop up to the lecture-hall. On their faces was an expression of collective long-suffering. Faced with this miserable phalanx, Professor Wickham put his clenched fist to his forehead: sometimes the names of his staff went clean out of his head, which was not really surprising, as he managed to ignore them for weeks on end. He seized hold of a rather glowering, dark young man, and triumphantly brought him forward.

32

'Mervyn Raines, our Australian literature specialist.'

'Merv,' said the glowering figure. 'G'day.'

'Most interesting,' said Professor Belville-Smith. 'Australian literature. You must tell me about it. I have revealed my ignorance most sadly since I arrived here. I must confess that until I came, I wasn't aware . . .'

'That we had any,' said Merv. 'I know. That's what all the bloody pommies who come out here say.'

'Bill Bascomb,' said Professor Wickham quickly.

'Good morning, again,' said Professor Belville-Smith. 'I must thank you once more for your kindness in rescuing me last night.'

'Oh, you've met,' said Wickham, indulging again in his odd gesture of knocking his forehead with his fist.

'Yes, thank you,' said Belville-Smith.

My God, thought Wickham, what did he mean by 'rescuing'? If he spent the night with Bascomb and that bitch O'Brien I can guess what the conversation was about.

Turning frantically around he hastily introduced the guest to Dr Day – 'our Victorian specialist' – a bleary-eyed figure whose entire skin area seemed to have been treated with nicotine, whose trousers were several sizes too big for him, and whose shirt was stained with a splash of red wine, and torn across the shoulder.

'What ho,' said Dr Day, as they shook hands: 'Been getting in a quick one before the lecture, have you? Wish I'd got a sniff of it earlier, I'd have been along.'

'Dr Porter, Mr . . . er . . . Miss . . . er,' said Professor Wickham vaguely, and began leading him out of the door up the hill. The rest of his staff trooped behind them in a somewhat disconsolate body, the unintroduced staff members at the rear, feeling vaguely insulted as usual. Professor Belville-Smith, clutching a disorderly mass of yellowing paper which he had extracted from his briefcase in Alice O'Brien's room, dropped them into the dust, and then retrieved them in dubious order. Alice had been right. He was, indeed, to lecture in a shed which looked as if it might smell of sheep-dip. Ranged along the front row of this unimpressive lecture-hall were Mrs Wickham, and some of her friends from the local minor gentry. The men had large stomachs, popping in and out periodically over their bursting belts: the women wore large gauzy hats, which swamped them. Professor Wickham performed the introduction to his wife with enthusiasm. Lucy usually made things right with people when they actually met her, however infuriated they might be with the things she did behind their backs.

'My wife Lucy,' he said, 'who's been so much looking forward to meeting you.'

Lucy Wickham was a plump, curvaceous, merry little creature with a heart of steel. She had a mass of black, lustrous, latin hair, and her glittering dark eyes oozed invitation. People assumed she had a mediterranean impulsiveness and generosity, but they soon learned otherwise, for when she wanted something, which was most of the time, she had the doggedness and immovability of a bulldozer. Some said she looked young, which meant that unlike most academic wives she didn't look more than her age. Her hot-toast-and-butter voice, shamelessly pouring forth outrageous compliments that she didn't expect the recipient to think were sincere, always disarmed suspicion, and even Professor Belville-Smith felt a spark of interest course through his elderly body.

This was something not all that far removed from the great hostesses of his young days (he had once been introduced to Lady Ottoline Morrell on a railway station) and he submitted with excellent grace to the introductions she performed, introductions to the local graziers and civic dignitaries who sat around her. This done, Lucy turned to her husband, whom she treated

34

on all public occasions as a troublesome appendage, and said:

'Bobby, do get on and introduce Professor Belville-Smith. I can hardly wait to hear what he has to say about Mrs Gaskell.' She turned to the distinguished guest: 'I *do* hope you are going to say something at least about . . . *Cranford*.'

The suspense before the title was killing to Professor Wickham. He still remembered the public occasion – it was that visiting American who left behind such convincing proof of his virility – when Lucy had revealed that she was under the impression that Ernest Hemingway had written *The Hunchback of Notre Dame*. Professor Belville-Smith reassured her on this point, and Professor Wickham went with his apologetic shuffle up to the lectern, and flammed his way through his usual routine with guest lecturers:

'. . . distinguished critic . . . sensitive insights . . . how honoured we are by his visit.'

This done, Professor Belville-Smith gathered together his papers, and walked up to the stage. Dimly he perceived, for his eyes were not good, the rows of check shirts and jeans, the well-developed girls in the bright flowered frocks contrasting with the general dullness of the front row. Common to all, though this he did not see, was the glazed expression of the unwilling audience, the uninterested audience, the over-lectured-to audience. Nor could he see that some at the back of the room were writing their weekly letters home.

Clearing his throat, he began with the familiar and well-worn words, which he had penned in his youth.

'To enter the enchanted world of Mrs Gaskell's novels demands from the reader of today no common effort. To pass from our world of telephones and motor-cars, of dirt and bustle, a world where one may eat breakfast in London and dinner in Paris' (so meaningless had the words become by now to their author that he would have been surprised if it had been suggested to him that this opening, penned in the twenties, might benefit from a little updating) 'into the never-failing charm and courtesy of her world of Cranford, with its maiden ladies, or into the hierarchical certainties of the delightful *Wives and Daughters*, is a privilege which only the sensitive and the tolerant can enjoy to the full.'

And so it flowed on. Even the diligent students put down their poised pens and settled into a dim, tranced state. The others sank further and further down into their seats. This was exactly the type of thing they had expected. Professor Wickham wondered if it would be noticed if he closed his eyes. Lucy Wickham leaned forward, apparently with rapt attention, but actually meditating vigorous measures to make apparent her displeasure to the lecturers who would be intruding on her party that night. One of her rural guests began to snore and she nudged him as if involuntarily with her elbow.

Merv Raines screwed up his mouth and whispered to Bill Bascomb: 'They don't make lectures like that any more.'

'Life must have been easy for lecturers in those days,' whispered Bill. 'That sort of muck just writes itself.'

So somnolent did the prevailing atmosphere become that not all Professor Belville-Smith's audience noted a rather remarkable passage in his lecture, which occured after about twenty minutes. He had torn himself, reluctantly, away from the maiden ladies of Cranford, and was dealing gingerly with the topic of Mrs Gaskell as social critic:

'Important though the subject of unmarried mothers must have seemed to her when she wrote *Ruth*; and important though the subject of the ills of industrial England undoubtedly was at the time – and indeed, is

36

now – it was not in those subjects that her true genuis displayed itself, and it is not to *Mary Barton,* or *North and South,* or *Ruth,* that the lover of Mrs Gaskell returns with anticipations of rare pleasure. For when the magic of her timeless Cranford world evaporates, she becomes – dare one say it? – a little pedestrian. What we remember her for is not the manufactured excitements of Mary Barton's attempt to save her worthy but dull lover, but the hilarious satire of her portrait of Mrs Bennet. Many have felt Jane Austen's satire of Elizabeth's mother unkind – nay, even cruel. But here I would beg to differ . . .'

At this point a slightly puzzled frown wafted briefly over the face of Professor Belville-Smith. He gazed at his notes. Had something happened? But the familiar words exerted their usual drug-like spell, and he continued for a further half-hour with his well-known attempt to rob Jane Austen of malice, intelligence and common-sense. His audience did not all adapt so easily to the change of subject.

'Silly old bugger's muddled his notes,' whispered Bill Bascomb to Alice O'Brien.

'Doesn't make much difference as far as I can see,' she whispered back. 'It's all a load of garbage.'

'True,' whispered Bill. 'But it's supposed to be Jane Austen tomorrow. Will we have to sit through it all again, or do you think he'll manage to switch back to Mrs Gaskell?'

The lecture came gently but rhetorically to an end – for Professor Belville-Smith was rather proud of his perorations – and so did the polite applause. Professor Wickham shuffled again to the stage and said – as he always did – that the lecture had given them all a lot to think about, just as if he hadn't stopped thinking on academic subjects twenty years before. The students drifted off towards their dining halls, and Professor Wickham and Lucy steered Belville-Smith towards the

Betjeman-esque palace which housed the administration; they were all invited to one of the Vice-Chancellor's walk-about lunches, where one stood up clutching plates of food chosen because of its peculiar difficulty to eat with a fork. The intellectual highspot of the English Department's year was over.

CHAPTER FOUR

Party: One

Lucy Wickham looked around her long sitting-room, and down into the sensible little black dress that she was bursting out of. Was everything ready? The furniture had been pruned, and little tables had been taken from the stack and dotted around the room with ashtrays and plates of standard goodies on them. There was the plate of little biscuits with the tinned smoked oysters on; there were the cheese and gherkin refreshers; there were the cashew nuts and the bacon pops. And on the dining table which had been pushed into a corner there were the glasses, Australian standard sizes, all hired from Beecher's Hotel. Was anything else needed?

'Just one glass when they arrive for the academics,' she said to her son Richard. Richard was ten, and premature beyond all imagining, and had insisted on officiating with the drinks for the early part of the evening.

'Just one for the whole evening?' asked Richard.

'Well, no. I don't suppose that's possible. But leave them empty for as long as you can.'

'All right. But I can't see how I stop them coming to ask for more. What should I say to them then?'

'Tell them you're not yet sure whether there's enough to go round. Say they weren't expected.' Lucy thought for a moment. 'And *no* spirits for them. Just the red wine. For God's sake don't ask them what they want — just give them the red as soon as they arrive.'

'OK. I'll give them the Oliver Twist treatment,' said Richard, and sipped a glass of sherry experimentally.

Lucy looked around the room again: cheese twisties, potato crisps, peanuts, pretzels. Would the Turbervilles be expecting salted almonds? She looked at her husband coming in: when there were guests to see it, she'd have to straighten that tie. He enjoyed these little public humiliations.

'Now, the academics, Bobby. If we must have them, you'll have to take full charge of them. If you get the first two or three over to the corner there, they'll probably all go there as soon as they arrive. That will get them nicely out of the way of the real guests, and they'll be a long way away from Richard and the bar.'

'Yes, dear, I'll do my best. But you can't trust some of them. That O'Brien woman just goes off and introduces herself to people.'

'Just leave her to me. I'll take care of the old man. I don't imagine he's the wandering type, so I'll keep him down this end. I'll introduce him to the Turbervilles and some of the nice people. If this O'Brien comes near I'll freeze her.'

'She knows him already, you know. They met last night — in Beecher's I think.'

'*Really*? Bloody impertinence, muscling in like that. You'll have to get rid of that girl. With her accent she's not fit to teach in an outback infant's school. Well, if she comes near, I'll just suggest she shouldn't try to monopolize — in Beecher's I think.'

Lucy walked over to the window. It was dark, and the only sound was of semi-trailers, and the local yobs in their hotted-up cars. She looked out.

'No prizes for guessing who will arrive first. Bound to be an academic, they're always so bloody thirsty. And pretty sure to be that bastard Day.' (Lucy Wickham was a miner's daughter from Western Australia, and in the privacy of her own home her vocabulary tended to betray her origins.) 'Why you keep him I don't know. He's the world's worst lecturer, and he's never sober.'

Professor Wickham tried to explain – as always when his wife seemed to confuse his powers with those of Ivan the Terrible – that it was hardly a question of 'keeping' him, since once he had been engaged he could hardly be sacked for anything short of rape or communism. But as usual, Lucy wasn't listening. She interrupted him:

'Bobby. He's here already. Now that really is too much. Five minutes to go before the time we said. For heaven's sake – you'd think he'd have the decency . . .'

'I'll do something with him, dear, don't worry.'

'You'd better, or I'll skin you. Take him into your study. I don't want him in here before twenty past eight at the earliest. Even then he'll be drunk by half past.'

Peter Day seemed to have anticipated her, however. His progress up the pathway was instinct with laborious concentration – it was the walk of one who knows that if he relaxes his vigilance for a moment he will sway or swerve. He kept his finger on the door-bell just five seconds too long, and Professor Wickham counted himself lucky that he did not have to catch him when he opened the door. With the fear of Lucy in his heart, he took him by the arm and led him into the study. Peter sat down firmly in the easy chair, and then looked round with an air of surprise and grievance. Clearly he felt he'd been had. Professor Wickham, à propos of nothing, forced him into a detailed conversation about the merits of the Ricks edition of Tennyson, and surveyed with despair the bloodshot eyes and the grubby shirt (he had been made to change the torn one, but though his wife tried to send him out clean, she could do little about keeping him that way). This is

41

what one gets for employing Adult Education lecturers who got their degrees at Leeds, thought Wickham grimly. His opinion of the man was not improved when Day seemed to cotton on to the game they were playing, and launched into a lengthy disquisition on some textural nicety from one of the Tennyson dialect poems, with incomprehensibly broad and lengthy quotations. He wasn't quite sure whether he was being got at or not. Sometimes he felt that his staff seemed to be taking a kind of revenge on him – but for what he was never able to fathom.

By the time Wickham led his captive into the lounge it was nearly half past eight, and Dr Day had sobered up considerably. He always sobered up quickly, which was why he drank almost constantly. Wickham noted with satisfaction that he pointed himself immediately at the party of academics, which Lucy, without his aid, had shunted into the far corner away from the bar. He hoped that she hadn't simply told them to go there. She was quite capable of it.

'Hallo, Alice,' said Day loudly. 'You've got a drink. Is this a drinking party, or did you bring it with you?'

Wickham went to get Dr Day a drink.

'Enjoy the lecture?' said Day to Mervyn Raines. 'Had the quality of surprise, what? What do you think we get tomorrow? The whole thing in reverse? Start with Jane, then half-way switch to the Gaskell? One thing about visiting lecturers: they make the students appreciate the lecturers they've got already.'

'Nothing would make the students appreciate some of the lecturers they've got already,' said Beatrice Porter, an acidulated spinster of twenty-four or thereabouts, a protégée of Professor Wickham, who engaged her because she was one woman Lucy could not suspect him of having amorous designs on.

'Alcohol does nothing for some women,' said Day, to no one in particular. 'Thanks,' he said, as a glass was

42

pushed into his hands. As he took his first gulp he caught sight of Lucy Wickham entertaining one of the local headmasters and a grazier's wife in the other corner.

'Christ,' he said, 'look at Lucy's dress. Practically inviting us to pop our arm down.'

Professor Wickham grinned nervously, and Bill Bascomb put his hand on Day's arm to stop him going to experiment in the direction he had indicated. There was still quite a lot of Englishness about Bill Bascomb. Beatrice Porter turned on the swaying figure.

'Do you have to come drunk and behave coarsely at every social gathering the Department has, Dr Day? Couldn't you save your drunkenness for your lecturing days?'

It was well known that one of the few things Day was sensitive on was the fact that the students sent a token force of two or three persons on the days when he was lecturing. Beatrice Porter prevented anything similar happening to her by the bluntest of threats about what would happen in the exam to those who were not seen regularly at her own lectures. When Peter Day seemed about to remind her of this, the little group showed signs of breaking up with strain. Professor Wickham desperately tried to keep them together by broaching to them a plan for the reorganization of the syllabus which had never entered his head until that moment. The academic group dutifully stayed around him, most of them looking into their empty glasses.

Lucy, meanwhile, her eyes on the window and the road outside, had caught the arrival of Professor Belville-Smith. She excused herself from the dull and decorous little group around her, and bounced to the front door. She walked up the drive her arms outstretched in front of her in a gesture of welcome she had copied from a post-war Anna Neagle film about spring or summer in one of the more exclusive areas of

43

London. The distinguished guest appeared to be waiting for the taxi-driver to open his door, and the taxi-driver appeared to be waiting for the stuck-up old geezer to get out of his cab. Lucy opened the door, and welcomed her guest in her best vein of fulsome flattery.

'We really are honoured, Professor Belville-Smith,' she began; 'we have been looking forward to this for so long.'

The old man's polite demurs were muffled; so convinced was he of the inferiority of everything in this country that he was beginning to believe that he did indeed confer on it a signal honour merely by his presence. He was not looking very well. His blanched face and cloudy eyes altogether suggested to Lucy a dim, snuffed-out frame of mind, as if he had taken five or six sleeping pills by mistake before setting out. Lucy guided him by the arm up the path, rubbing her delectable little body against his ('treat for the old idiot,' she thought to herself), and then steered him into the lounge. He looked round the smoky, noisy room, blinking like an owl. Lucy found out his alcoholic requirements, and thanked heavens they had not indulged in cheap Australian scotch. She poured him a fairly generous glass, hoping that he had not indeed taken sleeping pills recently, and led him to her little party at the notables' end of the room. The little circle opened out somewhat reluctantly at her approach.

'Mrs McKay, Professor Belville-Smith,' she said. 'The McKays have had a property here for three generations. Mrs Lullham – the Lullhams have one of the biggest properties in these parts. Quite like an English county, you know. What a pity you can't stay longer, so we could really show you what life on a sheep property is like. That's something you can't get any idea of from the big city universities.'

A vision passed before the blinking eyes of Professor Belville-Smith of dirty-brown countryside, of flies, of unshaven faces with large chins and hats down over their eyes.

'That would have been . . . delightful,' he said.

'And Mr Doncaster,' said Lucy, turning to a tall, distinguished-looking man, turning grey, with a bonhomous manner, 'the headmaster of the Drummondale School. We call it the Eton of Northern New South Wales. Ah! I thought that would make you laugh.'

It hadn't.

'I'm sure it's an excellent school,' he murmured.

'Oh, it is, Professor,' said Mrs Lullham. He noted the strong overlay of Kensington, through which the usual strangulated vowel sounds occasionally poked their heads. It reminded him of the young lady at the motel. Where did these people get their idea of genteel English? 'You should just see how it has changed our eldest son,' she said. 'Well, if you'd seen him before he went there, you'd have said he was a real rough Australian lad. But now.'

She didn't go on. Mr Doncaster would have liked to compliment her on her eldest, but the memory of the hulking youth, renowned for his complete illiteracy and the predominant foulness of his tiny vocabulary, made him feel that he could not do so without compromising his professional standards. He was grateful for the intervention of Professor Belville-Smith, who was used, from giving tutorials, to jumping into awkward silences:

'Do you . . . er . . . model yourselves on the English schools?' he murmured, vaguely. 'Or do you have something . . . er . . . something specifically . . . er . . . Australian, shall we say?'

'Broadly we model ourselves on the English schools, on the big ones,' said Doncaster, impressively, in his headmaster's voice. But we do try to bring something new. Rural subjects, for example. They seem more, well, relevant here, perhaps. But in the more academic subjects we do have some difficulty in keeping up the standards. We rely a lot on people from England there, you know. People who are looking for the bigger opportunities Australia has to offer. Quite a lot who think the old country's on the decline, you know.'

Professor Belville-Smith snuffled a little. He wasn't sure that he liked that sort of talk.

'You are English yourself, I can hear. May I ask what school you . . . er . . .'

It was a question Mr Doncaster always hated, but he put his mouth into a forced smile:

'Charrington,' he said, naming a nineteenth-century establishment of little distinction.

'Ah yes. We have had some boys at St Peter's from Charrington, I believe. Quite a good *sporting* school, I'm told.'

'Quite good,' said Doncaster noncommittally.

At this moment Lucy Wickham caught out of the corner of her eye the figure of Alice O'Brien, heading for the drinks corner, and maliciously decided to frustrate her.

'Alice,' she said, gazing at her loud scarlet and orange frock of unfashionable length, and her peeling face with the too blatant make-up. 'So glad you could come. How *nice* you look tonight. But then you *always* look so nice, of course.'

Alice gritted her teeth and wondered whether to hand Lucy the empty glass and demand a re-fill. No. Perhaps later. Or perhaps when she became permanent.

'Beaut party,' she said chattily in her broadest Australian voice. She knew that Lucy would not be able to sustain conversation long in that style. 'Nice home you've got, too.'

Lucy was struck dumb by the directness of the hint: Miss O'Brien had been on the staff two years, and this was the first time she had been invited to the Wickhams'. Conscious that she was not at her best with animals that would defend themselves, she retreated.

'I'm glad you like it,' she said, and turned back, defeated, to the Professor. She would have to leave it to Richard to defend the stocks of alcohol against Miss O'Brien.

More guests drifted in. The Turbervilles arrived late, and with an air of considerable condescension. They didn't mix much with the University set. Once you got in with that sort of crowd, they said to their friends, you never knew where it might end. Lucy went over to them, bursting with pleasure, and led them across to Professor Belville-Smith as if they were well-bred poodles. Their clothes were well-cut, and almost hid the fact that they were fat. Nothing could hide the fact that they were stupid. Mr Turberville (OBE for services rendered to anti-Communism) started talking to Belville-Smith about the drought. It was not an ideal choice of subject, but he had talked about nothing else for two years, since the first intimations of a water shortage, and it was widely forecast that when it broke, a great silence would descend on the Turberville household.

The academic group, still deep in the entirely futile discussion of syllabus changes everyone knew would never be made, was joined by Miss Tambly, the head-mistress of the local girls' school. Built like a tank and dressed in a tent, she stumped forward and hailed everyone in her ex-Australian-army style.

'Evening all. Filthy weather. Hot as Hades and dust everywhere. Get me a good strong one, Bobby old boy.'

Professor Wickham bustled off to get her her scotch, and everyone insensibly stood a little to attention, except Dr Day, who was reminiscing to the bookshelves about amorous experiences on his Adult Education Circuit back in Sheffield, and was beyond standing to attention.

'God, I'm tired,' said Miss Tambly.

'Had a hard day?' asked Dr Porter.

'Those goddam sluts,' said Miss Tambly, referring to

the scholars of the Methodist Ladies' College. 'Have to parade the corridors with a gun soon to keep them in at night. Nothing but men, men, men, on their minds, morning, noon and night.'

'Doesn't sound any different from a University College,' said Dr Porter. 'And we can't lock them up. At least, not during the day.'

'Mistake ever to let men into the University,' said Miss Tambly.

'Quite right,' said Bill Bascomb. 'Same with the army, don't you think?'

Miss Tambly looked at him to see if he was joking. This was something she didn't like about academics: you never quite knew.

'Don't know about that,' she said carefully. 'Men know their place in the army.'

'Better not ask where *that* is,' said Alice O'Brien.

On the surface it was just a normal academic party.

CHAPTER FIVE

Party: Two

It was getting late, and Professor Belville-Smith was beginning to feel it would soon be time to go back to the motel. The conversation of the local squirearchy was no less intelligent, entertaining or subtle than its equivalent would be at home, but it was different, and though in his earlier days he had been used to being bored by people with money, had rather liked it in fact, still, the differences in the subject-matter were disconcerting, and made it more difficult to put in the right automatic responses. He supposed it was understandable that nobody at home would talk for any length of time about droughts, but now here was this woman – Turberville was it? – with her Queen-Mother blue dress and her Queen-Mother plump figure, going on and on, on the subject of reds. The reds teaching in our schools, the reds indoctrinating our fine young people in our universities, the reds who came over as assisted migrants, and the Australian Labour Party being, as everyone knew, just a front for Moscow.

Mrs Turberville's words were by now very near to being meaningless to Professor Belville-Smith. The two whiskies which Lucy had poured for him – contriving to ignore some other empty glasses, he was gratified to notice – had at first sat warmly on his stomach, and perked him up considerably. Now, however, they seemed to be waging war with the sleeping tablets he had taken before his afternoon nap, and his brain was playing odd tricks on him. Every time the word 'red' was spat into the conversation it exploded in his brain, like a glorious firework, with shades of pink and orange and scarlet. When he tried to pull himself together and reminded himself that the woman was talking about politics, odd names from the past kept obtruding themselves – Rosa Luxemburg, Joseph Stalin, to whom, for some reason, his brain insisted on attaching the label 'our gallant ally' – and he managed to summon up no names or ideas from more recent experience. Could it be, he asked himself in the back of his mind, that he was getting drunk? With one hand he gripped the back of the chair, with the other he gripped his glass. Gratefully he registered that someone was stemming the tide of Mrs Turberville's red menace.

'I don't suppose Professor Belville-Smith will be very well up with the political situation here in Australia,' said Mr Doncaster, in a gallant attempt.

'It's the same in England,' said Mrs Turberville. 'Worse! Look at the Unions there! And the Labour Party. You don't really think that George Brown could ever have become Foreign Secretary except on orders from Moscow, do you? Don't be naive. And now Enoch's gone, there's no one with an ounce of backbone in the Conservative Party.'

At this point Professor Belville-Smith was grateful for a slight interruption. He had not seen the Wickham off-spring before, a freckled boy with devil written all over him. He didn't much like boys. This one was now tugging at his mother's arm, with intended mischief oozing from every pore.

'Mummy! Mummy! Dr Day says that if I don't let him have a gin and tonic he'll have the balls off me in no time.'

'Richard!'

'Well, that's what he said, Mummy. I don't know what he meant, but that's what he said.'

'Well, go and pour him one, dear, and then I think it will be time for your bed.'

'But he's an academic, Mummy, isn't he? And you said that the academics were only to have the cheap red . . .'

The rest of the sentence was lost as he was led away by the scruff of the neck, through the door and up the stairs. Lucy Wickham, who had been the champion swimmer of the Kalgoorlie Girls' High School in her younger days, was perfectly able to deal with her son on the purely physical plane.

Professor Belville-Smith was puzzled what to make of this incident. One side of his brain registered that the voice of Mrs Turberville had been only momentarily stilled:

'And it's well known, of course, that they always work through homosexuals . . .'

The other side of his brain registered shrill sounds of pain from the floor above. At this point he was conscious that the well-stratified party, which so far had been exactly what Lucy Wickham had aimed at, was in danger of breaking up. The groups were actually mixing. He found himself suddenly cornered by the drunken Dr Day, on his way back from helping himself to an enormous gin and tonic. His mind, by one of its usual quirks, had now reverted to the question of Tennyson, and he had a desire to try out on somebody an indecent reading of 'Crossing the Bar'. Professor Belville-Smith found himself once more in a state of complete bewilderment.

'Of course, I'm not saying I don't agree with a lot of what she says about the reds,' said Mrs Lullham to Mrs McKay. 'But she does rather go on, doesn't she?'

'It really didn't seem fair on the poor old man,' said

51

Mrs McKay, who, like Mrs Lullham, disputed the right the Turbervilles arrogated to themselves of being the leading graziers in the district. 'She really is rather vulgar. No idea of the time and place for things. I don't think he understood a word of what she was saying.'

'He's all right now,' said Mrs Lullham. 'Look, he's got an academic to talk to.'

'Do you really *like* academics, Peggy?' asked Mrs McKay.

Over by the bar Alice O'Brien and Bill Bascomb were helping themselves to quadruple whiskies while the cat was away. They were also congratulating themselves on having finally got away from the endless discussion on the syllabus.

'Anybody would think we were trying to educate the little darlings,' said Alice.

'Day's got hold of the Prof,' said Bill. 'Shall we go and do our familiar rescue act?'

'Mother's little helpers, that's us,' said Alice.

'Peter,' said Bill, taking Dr Day by the arm. 'You were telling us about that woman in Sheffield when you were with the adult education people. We never heard the end of that story. Come outside and get a breath of fresh air, and tell me the end.'

'Let me get you another drink,' said Alice to Professor Belville-Smith.

'Should I?' said Belville-Smith. 'I confess I feel a little . . .'

'Exactly,' said Alice. 'In this company it's the best way to feel.'

'You've got the right idea at Oxford,' said Miss Tambly.

'Have we?' asked Belville-Smith, looking pensively into the brown depths of his new whisky.

'Lock 'em up early, no girls in the rooms after ten, that sort of thing,' said Miss Tambly.

'I see what you mean,' said Belville-Smith, rather relieved at finding someone to talk to whose conversation he could make sense of.

'Any girl will be a slut, if you give her half a chance,' said Miss Tambly.

'Oh, now . . .' said Professor Belville-Smith.

'So don't give 'em a chance, that's what I say.'

'Of course, one of the points you've got to remember about our rules is that we expect the young men to get around them,' said Professor Belville-Smith timidly.

'What the hell's the point of that?' asked Miss Tambly.

'Well, we wouldn't like the . . . er . . . colleges to become too like prisons, would we?'

'Why not, in God's name? I know what I'm talking about. I've got experience of prison. That's how I got my present job. Keep 'em locked up. You know where they are, and so do they.'

'Well, it's a point of view, I suppose,' said Belville-Smith. He had known Headmasters and Principals of Colleges who went *to* prison, but he'd never before known one who came from prison. It made him a little apprehensive.

'We encourage outside activities,' said Mr Doncaster to Professor Belville-Smith. 'That's one of the ways we try to stick to the best of the English tradition. They keep animals, do survival courses, all that sort of thing.'

'Survival courses?' said Professor Belville-Smith, his brain making one of its odd leaps into liveliness. 'For if they are attacked by kangaroos, or koala bears, I suppose.'

'Something of that sort,' said Doncaster doubtfully, rather unsure whether the Professor was completely *compos mentis*.

'A pleasant relief from . . . from Latin, and such

subjects, I suppose,' said Belville-Smith with a drunken attempt at urbanity.

'All work and no play, you know . . .'

'Scouts, too, I suppose?' said Belville-Smith, whose brain had apparently jumped back into its groove of weary, distant condescension.

'I beg your pardon?'

'Scouts,' said Belville-Smith, with a far-away look on his face. 'The Boy Scouts, you know. That fine soldier Baden-Powell. I remember them being founded.'

'Oh yes, of course. Yes, we have our own troop.'

'There's nothing like the scouts for bringing out the . . . bringing out the . . .'

'Best in a boy, no,' said Mr Doncaster.

'Were you ever a scout yourself?' asked the distinguished visitor, his voice seeming to come from an immense distance of tiredness and memory.

'No, not personally,' said Mr Doncaster. 'Would you care to sit down? You look a little tired.'

'You can always tell when someone's been a scout . . .'

'What I can't understand,' said Merv Raines, appearing to push Professor Belville-Smith into the corner of the sofa by the tipsy sense of grievance with which his whole body seemed possessed, 'is why all the universities in England do American literature, and nobody seems to know that Australian literature exists.'

'Yes,' said Professor Belville-Smith, his eyes focused on the ceiling, his mind infinitely further off.

'But was there ever a more over-rated book than *Moby Dick*? All that fuss about a bloody whale . . .'

'Yes . . .'

'And yet there'll be a lot of people in England who've never even heard of Henry Handel Richardson,' said Merv.

'About ninety-nine point nine per cent,' said Bill Bascomb, who was standing by the sofa.

'Yes,' said Professor Belville-Smith.

'See what I mean?' said Merv. 'Just plain bloody ignorance. Do you wonder that we get fed to the teeth here with being the poor relation? Nobody cares a damn about us over there.'

'Yes,' said Belville-Smith. The conversation went on in this fashion for quite some time.

Dr Day sat in the middle of the rose-bed, picking a few late blooms, and murmuring tenderly to them.

'Christ, she was a marvel,' he said to a pale pink bush. 'You've never seen such tits. Well, she used to go to all the lectures they had there, and she got a bit of a name around the place. She always went up and talked to the lecturers afterwards. So I heard all about her before I ever set foot in the place. Peter, my boy, I said, that's for me. So when I got her home, I'd hardly taken off my coat, when would you believe it, she . . .'

'That's the last of the booze,' said Bill Bascomb, pouring a few drops of gin into his red-wine glass. 'Do you think we ought to be getting the old man home?'

'Not really our job,' said Alice. 'But he looks as if he should have been home hours ago.'

They looked towards the sofa, where Professor Belville-Smith was still seated, still gazing at the ceiling, and making little or no attempt to cope with Mr Turberville, who was patiently, but drunkenly, doing his duty by the old man.

'Trouble with a drought,' they heard Mr Turberville say to his empty glass, 'is you've got nothing to fall back on. You've just got the bloody sheep dying on you the whole time, nothing but skin and bone, and you've nothing to fall back on – see?'

'Difficult though we undoubtedly find it,' murmured Professor Belville-Smith to the chandelier, 'to enter the magic circle of *Cranford*, how rich are the rewards, and how subtle are the pleasures of those of us who are willing to . . .'

Bill Bascomb hurriedly drained his glass and interrupted this meeting of intellect and wealth.

'Professor Belville-Smith,' said Bill, 'don't you think you ought to be getting back to the motel?'

'What?' he said, starting.

'Back. Don't you think you should be getting back? You have a lecture to give tomorrow.'

'Lecture?'

'I thought you might be a little tired.'

'Yes. Yes, I am tired. Call me a taxi.' He stood up imperiously and looked around the room. 'Call me a taxi at once,' he said loudly.

'Of course, of course,' said Professor Wickham, bustling up from the opposite corner, where he had been the last of a long line of recipients of Mrs Turberville's monologues. 'I'll do it at once. I should have thought of it before.'

Belville-Smith focused upon him, and mentally associated him with some grievance or other from earlier in the day. His grievances were very dear to Professor Belville-Smith.

'Yes, you should,' he said severely. 'Call me a taxi at once. You have been most remiss. And tell the driver to knock up Smithers when we get there.'

Professor Wickham, already dialling, was somewhat nonplussed.

'Smithers, Professer Belville-Smith?'

'The porter, of course,' said his guest tetchily. 'Give me your arm, young man.'

This last was said with a grandiose condescension which was so overdone that Bill decided that the distinguished guest was by now very drunk indeed. The heavy pressure on his arm bore out the diagnosis. Professor Belville-Smith, however, was by now quite unaware of his condition.

'I'm not feeling very steady, young man,' he said, resuming his imitation of the Grand Old Man of Letters. 'Just age, you know, just age. I trust the night will be clement. The autumn nights of Oxford can be treacherous, most treacherous to a man of my age.'

'I believe the night is . . . clement,' said Bill, conscious of Alice O'Brien's sardonic gaze on him as he brought out the adjective.

They came to the hall where Professor Wickham was bustling around with coats and scarves; Alice opened the front door to give Belville-Smith a breath of fresh air, which he seemed to need. Outside it turned out to be a bitterly cold early autumn night.

'Where is the taxi?' he said grandly. 'It should be here. Negligence on somebody's part.'

'I'll drive him home,' said Alice. 'Just a minute while I get my car keys.'

'No, you will not, Miss O'Brien,' said Lucy, emerging from the lounge. 'We don't want any accidents. We'll wait for the taxi, thank you.'

'I can drive on a lot more grog than I'm likely to get my hands on in this dump,' muttered Alice to Bill, enraged. And to do her justice, she could.

The taxi drew up outside, and they led Professor Belville-Smith down the garden path, Lucy pushing Alice aside from his right arm. Lucy found the conversation a little bewildering. He was apparently reminiscing to Bill about a meeting he had had with Jane Austen at Winchester shortly before her death:

'Charming woman, charming. Sick, you know, very sick, but brave. Quite what you would expect from the novels, and most witty, even though she must have been in pain.'

Bill opened the door of the taxi, and they eased him into it, still talking, the others expressing their profound interest.

'You must let me tell you more about it some time,'

said Professor Belville-Smith. 'Now, I feel rather too tired.'

Bill spoke to the driver and told him to make sure he got to his room in the Yarumba Motel.

'St Peter's, driver,' said Professor Belville-Smith. 'And drive carefully if you please.'

The car moved off, and they all wandered back to the house. The party was undoubtedly breaking up, and tempers were frayed. Lucy found Peter Day in the middle of a highly anatomical description of a yellow rose-bush, and told her husband to throw him out. Merv Raines had found some cooking sherry in the kitchen cupboard, and was sharing it around among a favoured few.

'Do you think he understood the point I was trying to make about Henry Handel Richardson?' he asked Bill.

'Don't suppose he even heard it,' said Bill.

'Bloody pommies are all alike,' said Merv. 'And elderly pommies even more so.'

'Perhaps if you'd got hold of him before you were both pissed to the rooftops,' said Bill.

'I simply can't understand the need of some people to drink,' said Beatrice Porter to Alice O'Brien.

'What do you use – vinegar?' said Alice.

'Just like the Wickhams to let the drink run out,' said Mrs McKay, a little tipsily, to Mrs Lullham. 'They're only academics, after all, however much they try to hide it. It's not the sort of thing I'd like to happen.'

'Back to the prison-house,' said Miss Tambly to Mr Doncaster at the door. 'Still, makes a change to get out once in a while, doesn't it? See how the outside world lives.'

'Yes, indeed,' said Mr Doncaster. Since the Drummondale School was an institution of infinitely higher prestige than the Methodist Ladies' College, he felt compelled to add: 'I find the difficult thing, though, is to limit the number of invitations.'

'Funny. I've never found that,' said Miss Tambly.

'So glad you could come,' said Lucy Wickham to Mrs Turberville at the door, closely watched by Bill Bascomb. 'I wish you could have heard him tell us about his meeting with Jane Austen. Fascinating!'

By nine-thirty next morning Lucy Wickham had been immortalized by a further celebrated comment, destined to be quoted long after Drummondale knew her no more.

CHAPTER SIX

Body

Professor Wickham was giving a tutorial. Or rather, he was being given one. Every year he put Hardy as late in the term as possible, hoping that by then his first-year students would have become reasonably chatty. This was because he never could be quite sure which Hardy novel it was he had read. Whichever it was, it had left on his mind a vague impression of doom and landscape, but nothing much else remained. So he sat there, encouraging the students to tell him about their response to *The Return of the Native*, and letting his mind wander freely over his own personal concerns.

Lucy had been angry this morning. It had been a pleasure to get away to the University, even though she had only given him toast for breakfast on the grounds that they couldn't afford anything more. If you give a party, Wickham thought, you must expect the drink to go. It was quite unreasonable to get annoyed about it – but then, reason and Lucy had merely an occasional friendship of convenience. Someone or other, aggravated beyond endurance presumably by her lack of logic, had once again given her *Thinking To Some Purpose*, and now and then she would produce some scrap which remained from her reading of it to demolish him in argument. Otherwise her mind had been quite unaffected.

Still, at least the party had not been a total disaster. If Professor Belville-Smith had been bored, he had nonetheless stayed for a long time, and talked to a lot of people. This was an improvement on some of their other visiting celebrities. Professor Wickham doubted whether his own staff had shown up in a sparkling light intellectually, but then they never would. How was one to attract sparkling intellects to a cultural Golgotha like Drummondale? Only to someone with the mental level of Guy Turberville could his staff appear like brilliant minds. Still, all in all, he had known worse. Much worse.

He got rid of them at ten to eleven, and went to borrow a cigarette from one of his staff. He always chose one of the most junior members, and they regarded the supplying him with cigarettes during work hours in the light of a payment of tithes. They knew why it was, and in a way forgave him. Lucy was a very expensive wife. To their minds she didn't pay very handsome dividends, but then she might have talents they knew nothing of. As he let Merv Raines hand him two Peter Stuyvesants ('one for after the lecture'), and then let him light one, Professor Wickham inclined towards expansiveness.

'I hope you enjoyed the party,' he said.

'Real nice do,' said Merv, in his surly way.

'We must do it more often,' said Wickham, with a mental shudder in the direction of Lucy.

'Beaut idea,' said Merv.

There was silence. Somehow they never found much to say to each other.

'Better be getting up the hill for the lecture,' said Wickham, dragging heavily on his cigarette.

He fetched his gown, and started up to the lecture-room, chatting with such members of his staff as were

61

around about the previous evening. He was, as always, completely unembarrassed about his own or Lucy's delinquencies as hosts. Probably they had already passed completely out of his mind. Quite a short period of time enabled him to throw a haze of conviviality over the dreariest or most disastrous occasions. So he chatted on quite unselfconsciously as he walked with Merv and Bill Bascomb up the hill. It was only when he stood in the doorway to the lecture-theatre and surveyed the rather thin assembly there that a thought struck him. He turned around to his little band of followers:

'Where's Belville-Smith?'

Everyone looked at him.

'Didn't anyone go and get him?' asked Wickham, with his familiar gesture of banging his fist against his forehead.

'We thought naturally you'd be doing that on your way in,' said Bill Bascomb.

'I had a tute. Oh Christ in Hell. Stand at the door, and don't let any of these students out.' And throwing a glare at all his staff, as if the negligence was entirely theirs, he hared off down the hill.

'Mrs McArthur,' he shouted to the secretary as he went past the office. 'Phone for a taxi to go to the Yarumba Motel. Why do I have to think of everything?'

He picked up the phone in his room and dialled the motel. He'd have to make it right with the old man. Again.

'Yarumba Motel? I want to speak to Professor Belville-Smith. At once, please.'

The genteel voice at the other end answered calmly: 'I'm awfully sorry; Professor Belville-Smith has been found with his throat cut. Is there any message?'

On the little shelf by the outside wall in the room at the Yarumba Motel occupied by Professor Belville-Smith stood a large and well-filled breakfast tray. Coffee in a little jug, with another little jug of milk and two little paper pouches with sugar; three pieces of toast made from pre-sliced bread, with plastic-packaged portions of butter and marmalade. And a large plate of steak, bacon, sausages and kidneys, with two over-done fried eggs on top. It was not the breakfast Professor Belville-Smith had ordered, but he would never now get a chance to tell them so.

On the bed, pyjamaed, lay the body of the distinguished visiting literary figure. His throat had been cut from ear to ear, and there was a great deal of blood, red blood, over the sheets and the pillows. There was a large red stain on the wall, and another pool on the floor, quite spoiling the non-descript beige carpet. There was nobody to utter the obvious quotation from *Macbeth*, but sentiments appropriate to the play were not wanting. The cool, tanned receptionist in her tasteful floral print frock looked with mild distaste at the scene from the safety of the doorway, and said: 'Dreadful to think of it happening in this motel.'

And the motel caretaker, standing by the bed until such time as the police turned up, said: 'Not a very nice thing to happen anywhere.'

The rebuke went unnoticed.

'We've always tried to have things so nice here, haven't we?' the receptionist continued. 'Never any trouble with the police before, except that case of the manager and that girl under the age of consent, and he hushed that up, though it cost him a packet. Do you think he might be able to hush this up?'

'Not a hope,' said the caretaker. 'Might be if the chap was an Abo, but he's not.'

Now the receptionist really was shocked.

'I should think not! Watch your language! An Abo in this motel!'

'Hey, Fred!' shouted the police constable to one of a

63

little ring of sergeants playing whist round a table in the smoky back room of the police station. 'Call from the Yarumba Motel. They say there's been a murder.'

'OK. Tell 'em I'll be round. Just finish this game.'

'They say it's urgent.'

'Aw, it'll just be some drunk Abo.'

'No, it's not. They said it was some Professor or other. He was staying there.'

'Some egg-head, eh? OK. Speed it up a bit, Jack. Just finish this hand.'

'Isn't it *dreadful*,' said Lucy Wickham with ghoulish pleasure into the telephone. 'I haven't got any of the details yet, but as far as I can make out his throat was cut.'

'Poor old chappie,' said Mrs Turberville at the other end. 'Seemed so full of life yesterday, too.'

It was the first time for many decades that Professor Belville-Smith had been described as full of life, and he was not alive to appreciate it.

The little knot of sergeants and constables stood around the motel bed, with the caretaker looking on. The two sergeants looked at each other regretfully.

'It's murder all right, Fred,' said Sergeant Jack Brady to Sergeant Fred Malone.

'Looks like it, Jack,' said Fred.

They both looked towards the caretaker to see if he showed any admiration for their powers of deduction. He seemed, on the contrary, to be repressing a sarcasm.

'Poor old bugger hardly woke up, I wouldn't wonder,' said Sergeant Brady. 'Doesn't seem to have put up any fight.'

'He was about eighty,' said the caretaker. 'Would you expect him to do a swift bit of ju-jitsu, swing around from the chandelier, or something like that?'

64

'What the hell are you doing here anyway, smart Aleck?' said Sergeant Brady.

'Get lost,' said Sergeant Malone. The caretaker left them reluctantly, as if he thought they might bury the body under the floor-boards, and try and forget the whole thing.

When they were alone, they looked at each other again.

'It's murder all right,' said Sergeant Brady. Sergeant Malone nodded sagely.

'We'll have to call Royle, you know.'

'He'll be wild.'

'I know he'll be wild.'

'He hates being called when he's on the job.'

'I know he does. But what did he give us the phone numbers for? If we can't phone him when we've got a murder on our hands, what can we call him for?'

Sergeant Malone thought for a bit.

'If he won the lottery?' he suggested.

'Come on,' said Brady. 'Here's the list. Wednesday 11.30 – 12.30. Drummondale 4561. Are you going to phone him, or am I?'

'You are.'

Sergeant Brady sighed and went towards the reception office.

CHAPTER SEVEN

Inspector Royle

The job that Inspector Royle was on was Mrs Winifred Fairweather of 59 Bardell St, Drummondale, and she was just beginning to get excited when the phone rang.

Mrs Fairweather obliged Inspector Royle on Wednesdays at 11.30 with the full permission of her husband, Fred Fairweather, whose only conditions were that the inspector should be out of the house by the time he came home for lunch at one, and that whatever they might do together while he was out should not prevent his lunch being on the table when he came in. These conditions had been scrupulously observed, and the arrangement seemed to suit all parties. Fred Fairweather found it convenient to oblige the police. Not that his activities could in any way be described as criminal; but he had a small removal firm, and it was as well to make sure that the authorities would turn a blind eye to such small details as defective brakes or headlights or − in the case of one of his vans — complete unroadworthiness. So Mrs Fairweather had joined the list which included Mrs Jones (9.30 Mondays), Mrs Randle (2.30 Tuesdays), Mrs Ford (2.00 Thursdays) and Mrs Beecham (12.00 Fridays). She had replaced a Mrs Westerby, a widow with scruples who had been consigned to outer darkness because Inspector Royle felt she took more time than she was worth. Since Inspector Royle started paying his visits to the Fairweathers, Fred had stopped slipping small sums to one of the constables, so what one was gaining on the round-abouts, another was losing on the swings.

'Christ,' said Inspector Royle hoarsely as the phone rang. 'What a bloody time to ring.'

'Let it,' said Mrs Fairweather, putting her fingers around his shoulder-straps.

'Can't,' said Royle. 'Got a hell of a rocket last time I didn't answer.'

'When was that?' asked Mrs Fairweather. 'You weren't with me.'

'Oh, a long time ago,' said Royle evasively. 'Will you go and answer it, Win?'

'No, I won't. Do it yourself if you must. Bound to be for you. All my friends know not to ring Wednesday mornings.'

Royle lumbered off the bed and into the hall.

'Yes,' he said cautiously.

'Brady here, sir,' said the voice.

'You fucking idiot,' said Royle, exploding. 'What the hell do you mean ringing at a time like this? I've told you before. You've put me right off my stride.'

'Couldn't help it, sir. There's been a murder.'

'Some blasted black, I suppose.'

'No, sir. A Professor of some kind. Pommie, I think. On a visit here. We're at the Yarumba.'

Inspector Royle groaned.

'Christ in Hell. Not the bloody University mob. OK. I'll be right over.'

He slammed the receiver down with a force fit to disrupt the instrument and stumped towards the bedroom.

'Who'd be a bloody policeman?' he said, making a bad-tempered grab at his trousers.

'Worse if you was a fireman, I expect,' said Win, who was sitting on the edge of the bed and pouting a little.

'Number of bloody murders we get in this place you'd think it was Chicago,' said Royle, stuffing himself with difficulty into his trousers.

'Careful with that zip,' said Win. 'You don't want to do yourself an injury.'

Royle took his hat off the chest of drawers, and adjusted it carefully in front of the wardrobe mirror. There might be photographers around, and he could do with some good publicity.

'Will I see you later – after lunch, say?' asked Win.

'Course you won't. This is a murder not a bloody parking offence.'

'Who was it then?' asked Win.

'Some pommie Professor or other, unless Brady's got the wrong end of the stick, which he usually does.'

'English, eh?' said Win. 'Not really your business, is it? I mean, him not being an Australian. Couldn't they send somebody out from Scotland Yard?'

Rosy visions went through Win's tiny brain of including among her very special friends Inspector Alleyn, or even Lord Peter Wimsey. Royle followed her train of thought.

'Scotland bloody Yard,' he said in disgust. And when he went he banged the front door, and failed to achieve the nonchalant manner that he was usually so careful to assume when he left the various houses that he called at during the week.

He strode down the street to the car which he had parked round the corner – a touch more traditional than subtle. He was tall, heavily built, with dull eyes and a permanent midnight shadow. The criminals of Drummondale – about twenty per cent of the population – had a healthy respect for his fists and his boot, and none at all for his brain. But though he did not do a great deal to keep down crime, many people – and not just married women – were glad to have him around. For example he was well-known to the local publicans not only for his huge capacity with the beer glass, but also for his friendly readiness to ring them up before an after-hours raid. The local graziers found him very accommodating, too — but then, those whom they did not find accommodating never lasted long in Drummondale. He had a wife and two little girls in a weatherboard house on the outskirts of the town, but mostly he tried to forget about them, and they in their turn tried not to think too much about him either.

He eased himself into the police car, and put the key in the starter. As he drove off he groaned with his whole great body. Some University toff. Just the very worst kind of case. Now, with an Abo, you could just round up some of his friends and neighbours, thump the living daylights out of a few of them, and you'd have someone on a charge in no time. And with the graziers, well, you could come to some sort of amicable agreement. The trouble with University people was that you couldn't thump them and they couldn't afford to bribe you. Most of them were so feeble, anyway, that if you tried to thump them they'd collapse in a dead heap on the floor. But in any case, it wasn't worth it. He'd tried it once when he first arrived, but never again. There had been letters in the *Australian* and the *Nation*, questions asked in State Parliament, and a protest meeting organized by the Civil Liberties people. He'd been reprimanded by his superiors for that little lark. True, they'd winked while they did it, but it had gone down on his record, and he'd had to give up the practice entirely for some months. It might even have put back his promotion. No, there wouldn't be any thumping this time. But then, how else was he to find out who did it?

He drove the police car past the reception office of the Yarumba Motel and over to the doorway which Sergeant Brady was standing in. Some of the other cabins also had people in their doorways, or peering out of their windows, showing that the good news had travelled fast. Royle looked down to see that his dress was properly adjusted, and got heavily out of the car. He looked at Brady vindictively.

'It's coming to something, it really is,' he muttered. 'When a chap can't even have a quick naughty without being pestered and . . . Oh my Christ.'

He had brushed past his sergeant into the room, and was now surveying the feeble old body and the blood-stained bed, with the spurt on the wall over the reading light, and the red-brown stain on the carpet. It was the sort of thing that he rather enjoyed on TV, but it wasn't the sort of thing he'd come across much in real life. Murders he had known of course, in plenty. He often said proudly that Australia was the country for murders. He'd been on a couple of cases where husbands had found their wives in bed with another man, and done them in; then there was the man who ran down his mother-in-law when she was coming home from a bridge party, only the old monster didn't die, and recognized the car; and of course there had been several knife fights after the pubs closed. All these had been beautifully clear-cut. Royle knew, instinctively, that this case was going to be different.

'Well, what have you done?' he said to the two sergeants, who were watching him with dogged devotion, or something, in their eyes.

'Well, nothing really, sir. We were rather waiting for you . . .'

'Christ, you'll be wanting me to put you on the potty next.'

'To tell you the truth, sir,' said Sergeant Brady slowly, 'we weren't quite sure what to do.'

They watched him closely. To tell the truth, nor was Inspector Royle sure what to do. One thing was clear. His experience was not likely to come in handy in this case – any more than his usual methods were likely to be useful. He tried to cast his mind back to all those television serials, those *Perry Masons* and those *Mannixes*, watched in a haze of beer and post-prandial somnolence.

'Get on to the station,' he said finally. 'We'll want a doctor and a fingerprint man.'

Three hours later Royle decided that, surprisingly, they were making progress. He was wondering, in fact, if he might not cut a figure in the national press, perhaps be asked to write a short article for one of the Sundays. True, there had been no fingerprints in the room (devilish cunning of the murderer, that, Royle thought) except those of the victim himself and the cleaning-lady. But he thought he knew how the killer had got in, and that was something.

The motel backed on to a vacant block, where the council was proposing to erect a tourist office – happily oblivious to the fact that tourists only went where there was something to see. The bathroom of Professor Belville-Smith's room looked out on to this block, and had a long, fairly low window, which it would be easy enough to climb into and out of. Some traces of dirt had also been found on the sill. Now this last piece of evidence, which Inspector Royle was particularly proud of, and was not exactly conclusive, since the cleanliness of the Yarumba Motel was only of the obvious and superficial kind which is nowhere near godliness, but still it indicated a probability. He could make a good deal of it when he reported to his superiors. Now all that remained to do, he reflected with considerable self-satisfaction, was to find out who it was who had climbed in and out. That was the rub. If any of the police who should have been patrolling the town had noticed anything suspicious of that sort, word would surely have got to him by now. Anyway he happened to know they had been occupied with a darts marathon at the station, for he had seen the scores all over the walls of the games room when he reported for duty that morning. When they really got involved in something big they tended to forget entirely that they were supposed to be on patrol.

He decided to go and talk to the girl in reception. This was just what she had hoped, since she was meeting her boy-friend that night, and wanted to have all the latest details. She had been following every sign of activity across the courtyard with great interest from her window, but when Royle banged into her office she was sitting decorously at her desk answering correspondence. She had decided that brisk efficiency was the best way of meeting him.

'Oh, Inspector,' she said. 'You've finished now, I hope.'

'Not nearly, miss, not nearly,' said Royle impressively, sizing her up casually, but not in the light of a suspect.

'That's most inconvenient,' said the girl. 'Now we won't be able to let the room tonight.'

'Christ, woman,' said Royle, throwing off his majesty-of-the-law pose, and reverting to his usual self in the surprise of finding someone more stupid and insensitive than himself. 'Are you off your rocker? You won't be letting that little slaughter-house for quite some time to come, I can tell you that.'

'There's no need to blaspheme,' said the girl. 'I don't know what the manager will say, I'm sure. I mean, who is going to pay for the room?'

'That's not my bloody look-out, is it? Now, I've got some questions I want answered.'

'I was off-duty, Inspector, so I saw nothing at all,' she said, looking as if he had made an improper suggestion.

'Would you mind just answering the questions?' said Royle heavily, 'then we'll be through much quicker.'

'Well, you'd better come through to the manager's

sitting-room,' she said. 'Police in the reception room would *not* make a nice impression on our clientele.'

She led the way into a bright little room with mauve easy chairs and a big bowl of plastic gladioli. Royle remembered it from the case of the manager and that young lass, which he had thought was a very nice type of case indeed.

'Now, then,' he said, taking out his notebook and making laborious preparations for writing in it. 'Who was he?'

'His name was Belville-Smith, and he was a Professor,' said the girl rather sullenly. She had decided she did not like Royle's type.

'What of?' asked Royle.

'What of? What do you mean, what of?'

'If you're a Professor, you're always a Professor *of* something,' said Royle, who had learnt that much since coming to Drummondale.

'How should I know?' said the girl, doubly resentful for the lecture. 'Something educational, I suppose.'

'Who booked him in, then?'

'Professor Wickham booked the room by phone a fortnight ago, and he drove him here on Monday.'

Professor Wickham. Royle knew Professor Wickham. Prominent Country Party supporter, him and his wife. The better sort of Professor, in other words. Took a sticker for his car when they had a 'Support Your Local Bobby' campaign a year or so ago. Had a cheeky bastard of a son. Still, could be worse.

'English, then, I suppose,' he muttered.

'Oh yes, the old man was English,' said the girl, not understanding. 'You could tell that by his voice. Very old-fashioned-sounding, if you know what I mean.'

'You met him and spoke to him, then?'

'I spoke to him on the phone. I can't say I met him, really, because he didn't get out of the car when he booked in. Professor Wickham did all that.'

73

'What did you talk to him about on the phone?'

'The silly old b . . . The old gentleman was a little annoyed on the night he arrived over the fact that we do not serve dinner. Got quite worked up about it, he did. Some people expect the moon, really they do. And he was quite nasty when I suggested he might like to eat Chinese.'

'He didn't eat at Professor Wickham's on the night he arrived here, then?'

'Oh no. Professor Wickham drove off again just a few minutes after he brought him here.'

'Where did he eat that night?'

'How should I know?'

'Anyway, that was Monday. What about yesterday? Did he go anywhere yesterday?'

'How should I know? This is a motel, not a YWCA. We don't keep a check on our visitors. We have a very nice class of customer, so we don't need to. Look, why don't you go and talk to Professor Wickham? He *was* his host, after all.'

'Don't try and teach me my job, young lady,' said Royle as he lumbered to the door.

But Wickham it is, he thought, getting into his car. God damn these university people.

CHAPTER EIGHT

Professor Wickham

Lucy Wickham was a woman born to rise to occasions. Part of her frustration was due to the fact that the lethargic country town to which she found herself transported (due solely to the fact that there had been no other applicant for the chair) offered her all too few occasions to rise to. Even the Queen had managed to avoid it on most of her visits to Australia, and there were few places in Australia of which that could be claimed. But whatever else might be said about a murder – and Lucy was torn between sheer animal excitement at the thought of it, and the feeling that it didn't give the town tone – it was certainly an occasion, and it brought out all her latent energy and unreasonableness. At the very moment Inspector Royle was speeding along the dreary flat road to the University cursing his luck, Lucy was on the phone to her husband for the fourth time that day, broaching her latest demand, in her best public-school headmistress voice.

'All I ask,' she said, 'is that you don't mention Peggy Lullham.' The voice took on the tone of a veiled threat, that tone which Professor Wickham had such a healthy fear of. 'Leave her out of it altogether.'

'We just can't do that, dear,' he said, patiently reasonable, and unreasonably patient. 'You know what they say in detective stories. If you tell the whole truth, and don't try to conceal anything, you have nothing to fear.'

'That's fiction, this is fact,' said Lucy. She thought for a moment, then added: 'That's England. This is Australia.'

'Anyway, what's it all about?' asked Wickham. 'Why is she to be left out of things? Last time I heard from you all your friends were thrilled to bits at the whole business.'

'They were, at first,' said Lucy. 'But some of them have been thinking it over. It's all very well to say "Back your local cop," but you can't slip them a fiver in a murder case. All the Press would be on to it in five minutes, you know what reporters are. Peggy didn't say why she didn't want her name mentioned. Or rather she said her husband wouldn't like it. But I suppose it was that shop-lifting business last year that's made her wary. She thought they might want to bring it up again.'

'Shoplifting! With all the money the Lullhams have got? You've never mentioned that before.'

'Everyone knows. Oh, it was pure absent-mindedness. I've never forgiven Darcy's for making all that fuss about it.'

'What was it she took?'

'A lamb's-wool coat.'

'She must have an infinite capacity for absent-mindedness,' said Professor Wickham, impressed.

'It was a *short* coat,' said Lucy.

'Anyway, it's impossible, and you'll just have to make her see that. Somebody's bound to mention her before long. One of the people here will, obviously.'

'If you had any control over them—'

'Or Doncaster. Or one of your friends. I can't see them all magnanimously forgetting she was there.'

The truth of this seemed to strike Lucy, and as he was letting it sink in, his secretary knocked on the door, and poked round it an excited middle-aged face. The English Department was quite the most boring department in the university to work for as a rule, since most of the members of it were too lethargic to play at University politics, and she was getting immense cachet from the secretarial sorority over this little business.

'Inspector Royle to see you, Professor Wickham,' she said. 'Shall I show him straight in?'

'The inspector is here, darling,' said Wickham, putting down the phone.

Royle was sweating in all the places a man does sweat in, and sweating obviously. He was drawing his regulation blue handkerchief round his bull-neck as he came in. It was a warm day, he was nervous as a kitten, and he had been deprived of his normal outlets. He was also in a very bad temper, but he was determined not to vent it on Professor Wickham. Wickham, as a Professor, was ranged in his social register somewhere between the gentry and the shopkeepers, and he was not going to get on the wrong side of him, temper or no temper. He looked around the sparsely furnished room. Bookshelves on two sides, Wickham seated with his back to the window, the Venetian blinds half-closed, to conceal the fact that outside the knots of students were gathering, hoping to see one or other member of the English Department (preferably Dr Day, whose lectures were several degrees worse than anyone else's) dragged off kicking and screaming to the Police Station. Royle sat down heavily in the easy chair on the professorial length of blue carpeting (two feet by three feet) and took out his notebook and pencil.

'Well now, Professor,' he said, 'I don't think I need occupy you too long this time. I'm just collecting the gen, so to speak. Putting myself in the picture you might say. Now, this old – gentleman who's been done in: he was your guest, wasn't he?'

'The department's guest, Inspector,' said Wickham rather nervously, 'the department's.'

The distinction took some time to sink in.

'Like, he wasn't a personal friend or anything you mean?'

'No indeed. Nothing of the sort. I've never seen him in my life before to my knowledge, unless I went to some of his lectures in my Oxford days, but if I did I don't remember them.' He rather wished he had not made this admission. 'Anyway, I'm quite certain I've never met him before on a social occasion.'

'So he wasn't a friend. Could you say he was here on –' the phrase was brought out rather proudly – 'academic business?'

'You could put it that way, I suppose. He was on a lecture tour. We often get people going round the country you know, giving lectures at each of the universities. The British Council sponsors them usually, or the Commonwealth Universities Association. Often they are retired English Professors, and such like, and sometimes very elderly indeed, like Professor Belville-Smith. He'd been to Perth, Melbourne, Sydney and so on, and he was due to go on to Brisbane today.'

'So he'd given his lectures here?'

'One. We didn't want to overstrain him, since we had heard he was – a bit on the feeble side, so he just had the one yesterday, and was due to give the other today.'

'You won't get any more lecturing out of him,' said Royle, giving way to his usual vein of humour. 'What about the other people here? The – lecturers and students, for example?'

'He didn't speak to any of the students,' said Wickham. 'On the whole we thought it better. We did think of arranging a seminar, but we heard from Melbourne he had some difficulty getting on the same wavelength as the students, so we didn't. Our students are not terribly lively at the best of times, you know.'

78

'Too bloody lively if you ask me,' said Royle, who was relaxing from minute to minute as Professor Wickham proved so notably un-uppity. 'What about your staff, the lecturers?'

'As far as I know he wasn't acquainted with any of them from the past. At least he didn't show any sign of recognizing any of them. But he was very old, you understand.'

'Gaga, eh?'

'Well, perhaps not exactly. Or not quite. But I do doubt whether he would necessarily have recognized anyone, even if he had had contact with them in the past.'

'So there's no reason that you know of to connect him with any particular members of your staff?'

'Not really. I do know he had dinner on the night he arrived with Miss O'Brien and Mr Bascomb. I believe they met up in Beecher's dining-room – quite by accident, I'm sure. But that's something you can check up on when you talk to them.'

Professor Wickham enjoyed this little piece of revenge. Inspector Royle noted down the names.

'I believe you said he was from Oxford,' he said cautiously, straying dubiously into this territory, as if afraid of revealing his ignorance.

'Yes, that's right.'

'Oxford, England?'

'Oxford, England.'

'Any particular address?'

'St Peter's College. I've wired the Master of the College about the murder, but so far there has been no reply.'

It was the first thing Wickham had done, and done with some officiousness. He found any contact with Oxford pleasurable and flattering, and he looked forward to prolonged correspondence with the Principal as perhaps a prelude to some closer contact next time he and Lucy had leave.

'Can you tell me which members of your staff have been to Oxford at any time?'

Mr Bascomb has. He has only just joined us. Graduated a couple of years ago. Still very young and . . . well, you know these English boys. I believe Dr Day was there for a year or so. Not as a student, though – as a librarian, or something of the sort.'

'Nobody else?'

'Not that I can think of,' said Professor Wickham, thinking hard. 'Oh yes, there's Smithson, but he was away last night, and isn't back yet. He had an external school, somewhere or other.'

'You yourself . . .'

'Yes, of course, I was there, as I think I said earlier. I went up just after the war, before I was married. All the ex-servicemen were up, so the place had rather lost its usual tone.' (It was one of his great regrets.) 'I got married there, and my wife and I were there for two years after that.'

'Wife too, eh?'

'Yes.'

Inspector Royle shifted himself massively in his chair at the thought of Lucy Wickham, whose name he had frequently had the notion of adding to his list of Royle's hostesses, prevented only by the suspicion that she might be out of his class. His mind ran along predictable lines of adultery between her and the dead Professor, but the thought of the withered old body in the bed came to him suddenly, and made even him hesitate. Still, perhaps twenty or so years ago . . .

'Do you happen to know what the old gentleman was doing last night?' he asked, dragging his mind back to the present.

'Yes, of course. He was at a party in my house. Given in his honour, you might say.'

'A party, eh? What time did he leave?'

'About half-past eleven, I'd say. We got him a taxi,

and put him in it, so you can probably check with the driver or the taxi switchboard. The driver was supposed to make sure he got to his room all right, but with that sort of person you can never be quite sure if he actually did.'

'OK. I'll check that. Who was at this party, apart from him? Academic people? University crowd?'

'Well yes, partly. Some of them were members of the department here, of course.'

'Of course.'

'Some private friends of my wife and myself. The Turbervilles. The McKays. Mrs Lullham.'

He brought them out as if they were patents of nobility. For Royle they were.

'I see. Anyone else?'

'Doncaster, from the Drummondale School. And Miss Tambly, from the Methodist Ladies' College, who came a little late. That was the lot, as far as I remember.'

'Do you think he met anyone else much while he was in Drummondale, or would these be about the only people you could say he knew here?'

'I don't know of anyone else. I shouldn't think it likely. He went to one of the Vice-Chancellor's stand-up lunches, but he didn't talk to anyone except the V-C. You know how he tends to get people into corners. Otherwise I think he mostly kept to the motel. He was very old, you know, and I suppose he slept a lot.'

'So this rather narrows the field down to your staff and the people at the party last night, doesn't it?' said Royle, with some pride in his deductive capacities.

'Well, yes, I suppose it does,' said Wickham reluctantly.

'Any little trouble there? Any little nastinesses?'

'None at all, Inspector. It was an extremely pleasant occasion which we all enjoyed.'

Professor Wickham said this quite sincerely. His

memory had already covered the occasion with a patina of elegant good cheer. Such retrospective optimism was one of his most invaluable assets.

'So sad it should end like this,' he added meditatively.

'Who did he talk to there?'

'Almost everybody who came, I think. Everyone mixed extremely well, you know.' Again, this was said without any twinge of conscience.

'Well,' said Royle, beginning to extract his bulk from the chair. The dark sweaty patches on his uniform had become still more obvious from the intense intellectual activity demanded of him by this interview in which he could neither bluster nor bully. 'Well, that's got the outlines clear enough. Now I can begin filling in the details. I'd better have a preliminary word, like, with your people before I go – the lecturers and so on.'

'You don't think, Inspector, that some marauder . . . some burglar, perhaps . . . could have. . . ?' began Wickham wistfully.

'No, I don't. Use your loaf,' said Royle exasperated, then he pulled himself up. 'Sorry, Professor. No offence meant. There was nothing taken, and nothing much to take. There wouldn't be any need to kill off a feeble old bird like that, even if he had woken up. It wasn't just a question of silencing him, stopping him rousing the place, like: they cut his throat, so they intended to kill him.'

'Yes, I see what you mean,' said Wickham. 'Still, there are some funny people about, you know.'

'Some kind of wierdo with a thing about old men, you mean?' Royle asked with a barely concealed sneer.

'Well—'

'We'll keep the thought in mind, sir,' said Royle, and escaped.

The rest of the investigations out at the English Department added very little to his knowledge. Not surprisingly, most of the academics said they went home to bed. No way of checking that at all, though the neighbours might be asked whether they saw cars coming in, and what time it was. Not likely to be much joy there at that time of night, but it was a slim hope. The exception was Bill Bascomb. Royle had had great hopes of Bascomb, since his name had come up twice in the conversation with Wickham. That was enough to make him suspicious in Royle's not very bright eyes. Meeting him for the first time he looked more unappetizing than suspicious. A spotty chap, not long out of short pants in Royle's eyes, and very obviously English, which didn't send his stock up. What was more he had obviously heard from someone that all Australian policemen were corrupt. This was true enough, though it did not stop Australians treating their police with respect, albeit a respect tinged with jocularity. Bill Bascomb seemed to be treating him merely as a joke. His doings after the party were rather different from the others'. He had had a lecture from Lucy Wickham for half an hour after Professor Belville-Smith had been shipped back to his motel on The Whole Duty of Lecturers:

'Which consists of being not seen and not heard,' he said, in what Inspector Royle regarded as his clever-clever Pommie way.

'I see, sir. And what did you do next?'

'Well, after the silly bitch let me go—'

Inspector Royle could not let that pass:

'Mrs Wickham is a highly respected member of this community, sir,' he said.

'Really? What very odd standards your little community must have, Inspector,' said Bascomb.

'Just cut out the smart-alecky stuff, and tell me what you did last night, will you?' said Royle exasperated.

'When the lecture finished, I asked Mrs Wickham if I was free to go now, and whether I could phone for a taxi from her house,' said Bascomb in an exaggerated schoolboy style.

'You didn't drive to the party?'

'Yes, I did. But I thought I'd had a bit too much to drink to drive home.'

Self-righteous bloody Pommie, thought Royle. You could tell he hadn't been out here long.

'Very commendable I'm sure, sir,' he said.

'When we got back to Menzies College – oh, by the way, I'm moral tutor out there, to E block. For the moment, anyway. I'm supposed to sort of Auntie Marge them. Well, when I got back to Menzies there was a party on in one of the corridors, and I went to investigate it, because it was after midnight by then. And I sort of stayed on, you see. I don't know how long, but an awfully long time.'

'When did you get to bed?'

'I don't remember, Inspector. In fact, I rather think I must have been put to bed.'

Royle looked at him closely. If ever a story was borne out by a face, this one was. The naturally unwholesome complexion had a greenish tinge, the teeth were stained with cheap red wine, and the eyes were dull and bloodshot. Perhaps he didn't look quite so dreadful normally, then. In an odd way Royle felt better disposed towards him. Clearly with a bit of training Bascomb would become a man who could take his grog.

'You drank red wine at this party, I'd guess, sir,' he said, attempting friendliness.

'Yes. Tuppenny headache. Never again.'

'You'll soon get used to it,' said Royle. 'If we can get this confirmed, it looks as if you're in the clear.'

From Bascomb and the rest he got fragments of the Professor's conversation during the evening, and a very strange evening it seemed to him to be. He was used to parties where men assembled down one end of the room around the beer keg, and the women talked about plastic nappies and the price of frozen peas at the other end. That was what parties essentially were, for Royle.

This didn't seem to have been that sort of a do at all. Effeminate, these academics, he thought.

Nor did it seem to have been quite the happy event Professor Wickham had remembered with such affection. In fact, almost none of the staff seemed to have enjoyed it, and almost all of them seemed to have a grudge of one kind or another. These grudges appeared to centre on Lucy Wickham, whose position as a respected member of the community Royle soon got tired of going into the lists in defence of. He recognized a right bitch when he heard of one, even if she was on the Country Party social committee. The exception to most of these generalizations was, as usual, Dr Day, who was every policeman's idea of a nightmare witness.

'Don't remember a thing,' he said genially. 'Never do. Don't go to parties to take notes, or write books, or save up things for use later. I think I got there a bit early, because Wickham kept me in his study talking some rot or other for half an hour or so. Lucy must have put him up to that. Felt really down when we came out, so it must have been long enough to sober up.'

'You'd had something to drink before you went to the Wickhams'?'

'You don't know the Wickhams' parties, or you wouldn't ask. Of course I did. You don't know how much you're going to get with them. When we went into the party Lucy tried to keep us from the booze, bless her well-covered heart, but she didn't succeed.'

'And you don't remember anything else?'

'Not a thing. Something may come back later – it sometimes does. Wait a minute – I think I was in the garden part of the time. Yes, I'm sure I was.'

'With Professor Belville-Smith?'

'Oh no, I don't think so. He looked as though a breath of fresh air would blow him away. I was probably pissing on the roses. Go and see if they're flourishing. At home we've got the best rose-bed in Drummondale, and that's what I put it down to.'

'When did you get home?'

'Haven't the foggiest. You know how it is. Ask the wife – she may have woken up.'

'Wasn't she at the party, then?'

'Not on your life. She and Lucy have fallen out – or rather they never fell in. If there's one thing Lucy dislikes more than academics, it's academics' wives. Consequently she always manages to freeze them off, right from the first.'

'Did you drive yourself home?'

'I suppose so. Yes, I must have. The car was outside this morning, without a dent in it, too. It's a good car – more or less takes *me* home after a party.'

So there it was. All but Bascomb without a shred of an alibi, and his needed close checking. If Belville-Smith had been done in at some time between midnight and five a.m., as the police doctor had conjectured, then any one of them could have done it. The whole thing need have taken no more than ten minutes. Inspector Royle's elephantine mind made the logical leap necessary to tell him that he ought to try to pin down some motive which could have made one or other of them – or one of the other guests, though that didn't seem to him very likely – do such a savage thing. But nothing anyone could remember about the corpse's conversation on the previous night gave any clue as to which of them it might have been. Everyone mentioned, with great relish, the little set-to between the distinguished guest and his undistinguished host just before he left, but none of them thought any more highly of this as a motive for murder than he did.

'If Bobby went around murdering everyone who thought him a lousy host,' said Alice O'Brien, 'even you would have caught him by now.'

Royle chewed this over in silence for a bit, and

wondered whether to put Miss O'Brien down as a sarcastic bitch. She marched in on the progress of his thoughts, however, before he had properly sorted out the implications.

'If you want to know who he was talking to, and what they were saying, you should pump Doctor Porter, if you can bear the experience,' she said. 'She's got ears in the back of her head, and she stores it all up, to use later on.'

'Blackmail?' asked Royle, positively staggered by these depths of academic iniquity.

'Not in the criminal sense,' said Alice enigmatically.

'Was she talking to the old guy a lot herself?'

'Not that I saw. In fact, I'm not sure she spoke to him at all. But she was hovering near him much of the time. She never drinks more than a thimbleful herself, so that she can listen to the rest of us making fools of ourselves, and then throw it in our faces later on. She's a Fellow of Daisy Bates College, and so am I. They say she practises her spying on the girls there.'

Inspector Royle took a hurried leave of Alice, putting her down as the sort who sometimes made mincemeat of prosecuting counsel if you put them in the witness-box. He liked the sound of this Porter woman, though. That was the sort of witness a policeman liked – one who kept her eyes and ears open. It saved so much questioning, and comparing of differing versions.

Dr Porter was very young to be a Doctor, but nobody ever thought so. She was ageless, and so completely sexless, that she gave even Royle the feeling that he was in some way bandaged tightly from head to toe in her presence. Her lips were compressed, her eyes were sharp, and Royle had no doubt that Alice O'Brien was right about her. But she was a respectable member of a respectable class, in a country which made a cult of respectability, and she intensely resented being interviewed by a policeman.

'I'm afraid I can tell you nothing, nothing what-soever,' she said, and she stuck to this line uncom-promisingly thoughout the interview. A clam was, by comparison, loose-tongued. She had not talked to the dead man herself, and she deeply resented the suggestion that she might have overheard so much as a word of anyone else's conversation with him No one who was a gentleman could even have considered the possibility of such a thing.

'But if you didn't talk to Professor Belville-Smith, and didn't hear what he was talking about to other people, you must have been talking to some of the other guests yourself.'

She gave a little silent nod of the head.

'What were you talking about?'

'We talked about academic matters, for the most part,' said Dr Porter primly.

'What sort of academic matters?'

'Reform of the syllabus,' she said. Inspector Royle simply retired, defeated.

Driving back, tired and frustrated, towards town, Royle saw the students of Menzies College streaming towards their dining hall. They lived in a collection of buildings like chicken boxes, scattered in a haphazard way around a more pretentious building, where they ate. Clearly the powers-that-be at the university thought eating a more important function than any other, or else the residential blocks had been built at a time when money was short. Royle drove towards the block over which Bascomb had indicated he held moral sway, and got out of the car. He went up to a little group of stragglers, and opened the interview with one of them in his usual way, by putting his enormous hand on his shoulder and lifting him several inches off the ground. Not surprisingly his initial questions about the party the previous night met with hostility, which took the form of complete silence.

'Look,' he said finally, 'I don't care a monkey's fart what went on at the party. All I want to know is whether this Pommie Bastard Bascomb was there.'

There was silence for a moment as the group inspected him, apparently wondering whether they could believe him. Surprisingly one of them decided that he could.

'Came about half past twelve,' he said, a youth who looked about Bascomb's own age.

'Did you see him come?'

'Yes. I was under the trees over there with my girl. He came in a taxi, and went straight in. I thought I'd stay out there in case he got shirty about the party, but he was beaut about it.'

'How long did he stay?'

'Bloody hours. He was enjoying himself.'

'What time did he go to bed?'

'About five. We put him to bed. Typical bloody Pommie. Can't take his booze.'

'You're sure it was five? And he couldn't have got up after he'd gone to bed?'

'Not a chance. He was bloody paralytic. He was so pissed he couldn't have scratched his own arse.'

That, at any rate, seemed conclusive.

CHAPTER NINE

Kenilworth

It was the next day before Inspector Royle got to call on any of the other party guests. He chose the Turbervilles first, probably from some obscure inklings of the rights of precedence, and he rang up Kenilworth in advance to tell them he was coming. Kenilworth was the property which Mr Turberville's father had bought from the grandson of a Scottish convict who had stolen sheep from Sir Walter Scott. He thought the Turbervilles would probably be a pleasant relief after a day spent with blood-spattered bodies and bloody academics. In the University world he was never quite sure what pose to adopt. Towards the Turbervilles he knew what his attitude and manner had to be: servile. He had always got on very well with them in the past. There had been the little matter of the youngest Turberville boy – the one at the Drummondale School – who had shot dead a jackaroo in a fit of pique during his summer vacation. It was easy enough to hush up that one as an unfortunate accident. Luckily the jackaroo was just out from England, an ex-Barnardo's boy, whom the Turbervilles had engaged on conditions not very far from slavery, so nobody asked any questions.

Then there'd been the occasion when Turberville Senior had run over that child and put him in hospital for six months. It was near the Abo reserve, so he hadn't been taking care, naturally, but by ill-luck it turned out to be a white child. What he'd liked about both occasions had been the frank way in which Turberville went about getting a handful of notes, large ones at that, from various little nest-eggs he kept concealed about the house in armchairs and drawers. He had handed it straight over without any embarrassment, and Royle had found the whole thing the very model of how a gentleman should behave. There was nothing he found so convenient as bank-notes. There weren't, he thought regretfully, going to be any bank-notes this time.

'No question of cash this time,' said Guy Turberville, as he and his wife waited in the huge lounge with the dull furniture and the stag's head over the door. He was a medium-sized, flabby man in his fifties with a military moustache and a rather weak mouth. He frequently sucked at a pipe, more for something to do than anything else, and he often lost his temper with his inferiors, particularly when things went wrong for which he knew himself to be responsible. That was fairly frequent these days.

'Of course not,' said Nancy Turberville, looking down her smart little navy dress and wishing that her neck was not beginning to look so scraggy. 'Why on earth should there be? We haven't done anything, have we? I know I haven't anyway.'

'No, of course not,' said Guy, looking around the room nervously, as if he didn't quite recognize it. 'It just seems the thing to do.'

'Silly habit to get into,' said Nancy. 'One day you'll do it to one who'll refuse and put you on a charge.'

'Never happened to me yet,' said Guy.

Inspector Royle drove past the semi-regal splendours of

the houses for the elder Turberville boys, past the Volkswagen used as a chicken-run and up the drive of the sprawling, much-altered-and-built-on-to colonial mansion, vintage 1895, entry to which was so dearly prized by Lucy Wickham and her like. He was immensely flattered by Guy Turberville's 'Walk right in, Royle,' shouted through the open window, and he came in to them rubbing his hands in a perfect lather of gratified subservience.

'Good morning, Mr Turberville, and g'day to you, ma'am,' he said. 'Sorry to have to break in on your like this.'

'Not at all, Inspector,' said Nancy. 'We know you've got your job to do, same as all of us.' The Turbervilles were very hot on the police doing their job when they spoke at political meetings, especially if there had been a hint of student unrest at the University. 'We're as willing as the next man to help you.'

'That's very handsome of you, ma'am,' said Royle, sketching a bow. 'Very handsome indeed.'

'Not that we can,' said Guy. Never saw the old . . . chap in our lives before last night.' He looked round at his wife, who backed him up by nodding vigorously.

'Well now, sir, that's what I thought would be the case. I thought: they won't know anything about it, but they will be unprejudiced outsiders. And that could be useful, I thought.'

'Ye-e-es,' said Nancy. 'I suppose you might say we were that. But of course, we'd have kept our eyes open more if we'd known. You just don't expect the person you're talking to to be bumped off by next morning.'

'But as it was, then, you didn't notice anything suspicious, nothing that you might have talked about together after the do, like?'

'Can't say we did. Don't remember that we talked much after the party, did we, Guy? Dull little affair.'

'You didn't notice anyone who seemed to know the

old boy from before, did you?' pursued Royle, looking at her scraggy neck with well-concealed distaste.

'No, not that I noticed. Poor old boy seemed a little bit . . . well, dim, to me, if you know what I mean. Not quite on the ball, so to speak. He wasn't up to much when he came, and by the time he'd had a couple — well! To give you an example: I was talking to him about the communists, see, and he certainly didn't seem to be very well up on the red menace to our free institutions. But that's true of all Englishmen. They're living in a dream world . . .'

Inspector Royle cut in hastily. He had been on the receiving end of Nancy Turberville's obsessions too often before.

'Have you been to Oxford, ma'am?'

Nancy Turberville was stopped in her tracks.

'Oxford . . . Oxford, Guy? Have we?'

'Blessed if I know, Nance. All those old places look alike to me. You're the one who insists on going. Quite happy at the races, myself,' he added to Royle, with an attempt to work up fellow-feeling. Royle smiled as if to say that he knew what womenfolk were like.

'That black and white place,' said Mrs Turberville pensively. 'Sort of patchwork. Lots of little souvenir places with ashtrays, and swans on the river and things.'

'Isn't that the Shakespeare place?' said Guy.

'I believe you're right,' said Nancy. 'Not Oxford, no. So I don't think we have, Inspector. And it can't have been for more than a day if we have.'

Royle gave up that line.

'Did you notice him talking to any of the academics particularly? Like it might be getting serious, you might say?'

'Well, most people had a word with him at one time or another. More a duty than a pleasure, I'd say, wouldn't you, Guy?'

'Didn't know much about the drought,' said Guy.

'Anyway, he seemed to get dimmer and dimmer as the night wore on, so that you were expecting him to go out any minute – ' Nancy Turberville gave a hard little laugh at her own wit – 'and then just before the end he got nasty with Wickham. It all blew up quite sudden, and I didn't really twig what was going on. It was as he was going, and he got sharp-like, in that English sort of way. Wickham's not my cup of tea, but I didn't see any call for it myself.'

'Other than that he had got on well with the Wickhams during the earlier part of the evening?'

'So far as I saw. Don't think he saw all that much of Wickham, but Lucy was talking to him a lot early on. Rather overdoes things, that one, if you ask me.'

'The hospitality?'

'The lot. She's a pusher, you know. Wants to get in everywhere. She's not really one of us, but she wants to be.'

'I believe she was at Oxford with her husband some years ago,' said Royle, with heavy casualness.

'Believe you're right,' said Nancy. 'Always talks about it. Trying to impress, or something. Her father was a miner, you know. A bit pathetic, really.'

'What about the others, the local lot, so to speak,' said Royle. 'How many were there?'

'Only Peggy Lullham and Joan McKay. McKay himself looked in when he brought Joan, but he was off to a meeting, he said. I wouldn't mind betting it was in Beecher's. All the Athertons were coming – parents, and both the sons and their wives – but there was something about a sick baby, so they didn't. May have heard there'd be academics there, of course. They're South African, and they don't like all this mixing.'

'Nobody else there?'

'Oh, Doncaster. Such a nice class of man. I can always find plenty to talk to him about. And that big woman from the Methodist School. Not so sure about her. Looks like a tank. Otherwise just academics. Don't get on with that lot myself. Just reds, most of them.'

'Couldn't agree with you more, ma'am,' said Royle. 'If you saw some of the things I see in my job, you'd wish the university had never come to Drummondale.'

'I do already, Inspector,' said Nancy. 'Place has never been the same since.'

'Don't know, though,' said Guy, like a rhinoceros in meditation. 'Gives the place a bit of tone.'

'Some tone,' said Nancy, in her most nannyish manner.

'So I'm right in thinking,' said Royle, getting reluctantly back to business, 'that you both talked to him at one time or another in the course of the evening – you on politics, ma'am, and you on the drought, sir – but you didn't notice anything suspicious, either of you. And you didn't hear anything odd in his conversation with anyone else.'

'No, Inspector.'

'Or anything nasty, like?'

'No, except for that little sput at the end of the evening. But that was nothing.'

'And you drove straight back here and went to bed?'

'Nance drove,' said Guy, rather smugly. 'She always drives us home after parties.'

'Never have more than five or six,' said his wife. 'Better safe than sorry I always say.'

'What time would this be, do you think, ma'am?'

'I suppose we'd be in by about half past twelve,' said Nancy, looking thoughtfully at her husband.

'About then, yes,' said Guy, not looking at her.

'Anyone awake when you got back, anyone who saw you arrive home?'

'What's the idea, Inspector?' asked Guy, going a purply pink. 'What are you trying to infer? I don't like your tone. It's coming to something when people in our position and with our good relations with the police need to have our statements checked up on.'

Royle hastily jumped in to set matters right, realizing that he had reached the limits of the Turbervilles' anxiety to help the police do their job.

'Just routine, sir. Just to get the old report sheet in order. Well, I think that should be all. Just to recap . . .' He looked down at his notes. 'You hadn't met the old guy before the party, you briefly talked to him there but didn't notice anything odd in his behaviour to anyone, you got back here about twelve-thirty and you didn't go out again. Is that all OK?'

There was a short pause.

'More or less, Inspector,' said Nancy Turberville. 'But there is one thing.'

If Inspector Royle had been observant he might have noticed Guy Turberville sit up tensely in his chair and cast a quick glance at his wife, but he was not, and did not.

'What's that, ma'am?'

'We met the old boy at the University, you know, the morning before the party. Went to a lecture there – on Mrs Austen, or some such person. I was thinking about my little granddaughter's birthday party most of the time, so nothing much got through, except that she was some English lady who wrote books.'

'OK, then, that gets things straight,' said Royle, making a squiggle in his book that he hoped they would think was shorthand. 'Anything else?'

There was silence, and Royle lumbered to his feet. The Turbervilles stood by the mantelpiece, and looked as if they expected him to back out of the presence. Royle blundered towards the door like a learner crab, and made his farewells, hoping, he said, that he didn't have to trouble them again, thanking them for their co-operation, wishing that all the witnesses he had to deal with could be as frank and open and generally lovable, and concluding by wishing them health, prosperity and eternal life.

'Only too pleased to be of help at any time,' said Nancy Turberville with all the sincerity of Queen Victoria welcoming Mr Gladstone back for a further spell as her first minister. Guy wondered if the renewed frostiness was really directed at Inspector Royle or at himself, and he found out when the figure of the inspector was seen easing its great bulk into the police car.

'By the way,' said his helpmate, turning to him, 'I just remembered when the inspector was talking. You went out that night after we got home. You thought I was asleep. Where did you go?'

CHAPTER TEN

The Methodist Ladies

Inspector Royle drove thoughtfully along the drab, dusty green road towards the Methodist Ladies' College. It was clear that he was thoughtful, because he kept within the speed limit, and had on his face an expression of acute agony, as if he were preparing to use a recently-broken limb for the first time. His mind was slow to receive new impressions, and still slower to palate the unpalatable, but it was at last becoming clear to him that this was a case that could not be solved by just pinning it on someone or other; it was a case that had to be solved by solving. The case, if it were ever to come before a court, would have to be absolutely watertight. The university community as a whole loathed each other's guts, but when they felt themselves threatened from outside they banded together into an impregnable mutual admiration society. Like a band of crows which has lost one of its number, they would indulge in prolonged lamentation and above all make sure of a nasty revenge on the cat who did it. It was all very different from what Bert Royle was used to, and he hated anything novel.

He drew up slowly outside a grim, walled building, something between a barracks and a lunatic asylum. If the high walls had not been there, the buildings inside would have enjoyed a view over nothing, for they had been built on a dry, flat paddock way out of town, donated in 1912 by a pious Methodist grazier who had lost his only son by beating him to death. Since 1920 or thereabouts the daughters of middle-class Methodists and others had there received an education infinitely inferior to, but – as a compensation – infinitely more expensive than, that provided by the state system. Here they had been drilled, marched to early prayers, and locked away from all knowledge of the opposite sex except what they could pick up at home in the course of the vacations. The vacations were long and hot, and the Australians are an outdoor people; most of them picked up a quite surprising amount.

Royle found a small opening in the wall and pulled a large, flush-like chain which hung beside it. There was a thunderous ring, and then silence, that silence complete and utter which is part of the great Australian emptiness. He waited fuming for some minutes and was just about to exercise his beer-arm again when a door opened at what sounded like a distance of a mile and a half, and he heard a pair of elderly feet shuffling hesitantly towards the gate. Minutes passed, till finally he heard a sharp little voice very close to him shout:

'If it's Mormons, it's no use at all you calling!'

'It's not Mormons, it's the police,' yelled Royle. 'I have to speak to Miss Tambly.'

'Miss Tambly does *not* like vistors during school hours,' said the voice, apparently still not convinced that it wasn't the Mormons. 'You'd do much better to come back later.'

'It's the police, and I have to see her now,' bellowed Royle, now thoroughly out of temper. It generally took about thirty seconds of less than complete obedience to put him that way. There was a pause on the other side of the wall.

'It's a *man*, isn't it?' said the voice.

'Of course it's a bloody man,' said Royle, outraged. 'Have you forgotten what they sound like?'

'There is *no* need to be impertinent,' answered the voice. 'Some of Miss Tambly's friends have very deep voices.' There was a further pause for thought, and then the voice said: 'I think I'll go and get Miss Tambly. I don't like making the decision myself.'

And Royle was left to gaze at the dirty grass and the dusty horizon, fuming to himself about the opposite sex while the slow shuffle receded into the distance. The consequent silence was eventually broken by a very different tread. Miss Tambly strode purposefully forward, like Joan Hammond at the 18th hole, threw back the six heavy bolts on the door, unlocked the three padlocks, and stood in the opening obscuring all Royle's view of the seat of learning behind.

'Do you really have to come now?' she boomed to the surrounding universe. 'It's damned inconvenient.'

'Yes,' said Royle snappily. 'This isn't a matter of a dog-licence, or a lost bicycle, this is murder. I'm a busy man and I have to see people when I can, and I've already waited twenty minutes to see you. I intend to see you now. OK?'

'Makes sense,' said Miss Tambly, in a tone which suggested she was not used to hearing sense from the opposite sex. She shifted her great bulk a fraction of an inch back from the gate, and pointed inside: 'That's my flat over there,' she said. 'Keep your eyes straight ahead of you, don't look to left or right, and keep your hands behind your back.'

Mesmerized by one who seemed an even bigger bully than himself Royle slipped apologetically in, and walked straight ahead, casting not a glance around him at the chaste surroundings he found himself in. Miss Tambly locked and bolted the gate, and then thudded quickly up behind him.

'Can't be too careful,' she said, apparently in explanation. 'Griselda,' she boomed in a voice of thunder to a buxom adolescent emerging from a side door. 'Turn your face to the wall and count a hundred, and don't let me catch you peeping . . . They smell you, you know,' she said, lowering her voice to confidentiality. 'They've got some kind of extra sense. They'll do anything for a look at a man.'

Royle felt awed at the feelings he must be arousing among several hundred girls, all presumably twitching their noses in longing. He wished there were some way of reciprocating.

'*Any* man,' said Miss Tambly, as an insulting afterthought. 'God knows how it's come about. It's this modern world, I suppose. I know I wasn't like that when I was at school.'

Royle felt pretty sure she was speaking the truth.

They arrived at Miss Tambly's flat, which was furnished with brown leather chairs, oak tables ringed from innumerable glasses and coffee cups, and tattered Persian rugs. To add to the gentleman's club atmosphere there was a bored-looking elk-head skewered over the door. Miss Tambly locked the door, presumably to keep the male smell within limits, and marched straight over to an enormous oak cupboard in the corner, which opened to display an awesome array of bottles, most of them whisky.

'I know what you'd like,' she said, selecting one. Royle, still not entirely soothed, refrained from telling her what he would like. She poured a half-tumbler, went towards the bathroom and made noises with the tap. When she came back there still seemed to be a half-tumbler full of dark brown liquid.

She's trying to get me drunk, said Royle to himself. He decided he was quite willing, until a horrible suspicion of why struck him like a blow in the belly. But he was flattering himself. Miss Tambly merely served herself an equally stiff potion and sat down among her brown leather in a ramrod fashion.

'Shoot,' she said.

Royle downed a fiery mouthful, hardly blinking, and then clanked the thinking machinery into motion.

'You were at the Wickhams' party on Wednesday,' he said. 'Is that right?'

'Right,' said Miss Tambly, sipping reflectively. 'Not often I get out, but this was a last-minute invite. One of those grazier friends of the Wickhams' fell out at the last minute, I suppose. In fact I wouldn't mind betting quite a lot did. There weren't many of that crew there. They're probably fed up to the teeth with visiting academics, and I can't say I blame them.'

'When did you get the invitation, then?'

'Tuesday morning. Lucy Wickham rang me – you know what hide she has. I pocketed my pride. I like a do now and then. Matter of fact, I was a bit cheesed off with that old goat getting himself done in, because I thought I might get into a bit of strife with the governors for being at that short of show. A current bun and an orangeade is about the limit to their idea of a party, you know – and then you have to have a prayer beforehand. But it shows how wrong you can be. As far as I can see they're tickled pink about the murder, though they don't say so. The chairman of the board paid an unexpected visit of inspection and never stopped talking about it. The rest of them keep ringing up to see how I am.'

'Do you know the Wickhams well?'

'I see 'em around. Bobby's ex-army too, you know. Gives you a bond,' she added with a touch of sentiment.

'But you wouldn't usually expect to get invited to their parties?' asked Royle, rolling the liquid around his cheeks.

'Good God no,' said Miss Tambly. 'You know the crew they aim at as well as I do. The six months' holiday on the Riviera every two years crowd. The third-generation Drummondalians. They don't send their daughters here, of course; if they did the drought really would be hitting them below the belt. If I see them in the street to touch a forelock to it's as much as I do see of them.'

'Did you know any of the others there?'

'I'd met most of the academics. I'm one of the governors of Daisy Bates College, you know. Gets me out of this hole, now and again, which makes a change. Nice of them to ask me really, because I'm not what you'd call the academic type. Have a bit of strife with the old spelling if the word's more than three syllables to tell the truth. They wanted an expert on security, though. So I see Miss O'Brien and Dr Porter when I go to meetings there. Dr Porter's coming on to our board next year if I can get her. She's got the right ideas about morals, that girl.'

'And the male academics?'

'Oh, I see them around from time to time. Dr Day is always in Beecher's when I'm there. Can't take his drink, that one. That twerp Bascomb was at dinner at Daisy Bates one night I was there – making filthy conversation with the girls, I don't doubt. Shameful giving someone hardly out of school a responsible job where there are girls around. Most of the others I know by sight. You get to know people in a town this size, as you've no doubt found.'

'What about the conversation at the Wickhams',' said Royle, who knew all about Dr Day and had already classified Bill Bascomb as more drink than women and wasn't going to reclassify him on Miss Tambly's say-so. 'Anything of interest that might give me a lead?'

Miss Tambly thought. Clearly she was hardly more accustomed to waking her thought processes than Royle, and he waited with a good deal of sympathy.

'The academics were talking about syllabuses most of the time,' she said finally, with some disdain. 'Don't know why they bother about that sort of thing myself.

103

Just lock 'em up and keep 'em at it, doesn't matter what, that's our motto here. Mind you, I got the impression they weren't taking it really seriously. I think most of them were bored, by the look of them. They kept edging towards the bar and Wickham kept edging them back. Whenever one started leaving the circle he'd throw a question at them. Very dodgy, he was.'

Royle was surprised. He hadn't given Professor Wickham credit for enough smartness to manage things like that.

'Then the graziers were talking about the drought, of course. Oh, and there was some talk about schools.'

'How did that come about?'

'Don't know. I came in in the middle. I expect one of those graziers' wives must have been going on about Doncaster's set-up, how marvellous it was, and all that.'

'You don't sound as if you agree.'

'They send boys on survival courses to save money on food,' said Miss Tambly brutally. She snapped her fingers so sharply that Royle spilled some of his whisky: 'And I wouldn't give *that* for their security!'

'Anything else?'

'Doncaster and the old Prof were talking about the Scouts.'

'Native scouts?' said Royle puzzled.

'Boy. Then there was that fuss at the end of the evening.'

'Yes,' said Royle, 'I've heard about that. What exactly did you make of it?'

'Not much. I'd got a fair bit into me by that time. I always have a few before I go, just in case the fill-up process is a bit slow. And with the Wickhams you can be quite sure it will be. So I tanked up on vodka – no smell you know – and by the end of the evening I wasn't functioning too good . . . too well,' she corrected herself. 'Oh, what the hell.'

'You didn't think there was anything underneath this

last bit of trouble,' said Royle, not understanding Miss Tambly's grammatical dilemmas. 'You didn't think it might be really about something else altogether?'

'I didn't think anything,' said Miss Tambly, whose ramrod stance had relaxed considerably, and who was beginning to look as if this was going to be one of those days. 'I tell you, I wasn't functioning like I should. I was trying to pull myself together to drive home.'

'And the old gentleman? What was your impression of him?'

'Gaga,' said Miss Tambly, firmly, saying openly what everyone else had implied. 'Completely gaga. Or else just plain drunk – you couldn't tell which. At this party, now – one moment he'd be there, next moment he'd be miles away. One moment you'd think you were talking to thin air, the next moment he'd come back with something quite sharp – then he'd be off again for minutes at a time. He'd latch on to a word and repeat it over and over again. Most of our governors are like that, so I know the signs.'

'And that was the first time you'd met him, was it?'

'No. I was press-ganged into some lecture or other he gave in the morning – bloody waste of time. That was pretty crazy too, if you ask me. Started talking about someone called Gaitskell who I'd never heard of, but before I finally dropped off, he was on about Jane Austen. But I don't understand these things. English never was my strong point at Training College. I was in the physical education line myself, you know. Anyway I was thinking about a new kind of alarm system for the girls' dorm, so you'd better get one of the academics to explain the finer points of the lecture.'

'And there's nothing else you can think of, nothing likely to help me?' asked Royle, shifting his bulk around preparatory to heaving it up. There was a long pause.

'At the moment all I can think of is another drink,' said Miss Tambly. 'Have one.'

Royle passed his glass and settled down in his chair again.

Driving away from the Methodist Ladies', not smelling particularly Methodist, Royle drove as badly as he always did after he had had a few, but he was quite unconscious of it. Two of Miss Tambly's whiskies were quite a few of anyone else's, so it was surprising that as he approached the town he should recognize the figure of Bill Bascomb, going in the direction of college. He was carrying a bulging plastic bag from which protruded two large flagons of sherry and not much else. Remembering something he'd been turning over in his mind, Royle pulled up and opened the passenger door.

'Want a lift to the Uni?' he said with an approach of pleasantness. 'I'm going that way myself.'

'Don't mind,' said Bill, considerably surprised. He scrambled in, wondering whether it was the done thing to get in the back or front, and deciding he'd probably done right to get in beside the driver. He settled down in his seat, nursing his plastic bag. 'I had a couple of beers at Beecher's, so I left the car in town.'

'Really?' said Royle, suppressing a sarcasm. A smell reached Bascomb that suggested that he might just as well have driven himself home.

'Been to a party?' he asked.

'A Methodist one,' said Royle. 'You'd be surprised. Anyway, cut out the back-chat. I want to ask you something.'

'I thought so,' said Bill. 'I didn't associate the Australian police with giving compassionate lifts, somehow. Haven't we been over it all pretty thoroughly by now?'

'Yes, I don't want to go into any more details. In fact, I've looked into your story and as far as I can see, you're completely in the clear.'

'Glad to hear it,' said Bill. 'I was beginning to wonder

if they'd done away with the rope in New South Wales.'

'The only one that *is* in the clear, I may say,' said Royle pompously. 'The others have holes feet wide in their statements. That's why I thought you might be able to help me.'

'Always glad to oblige,' said Bill. Royle slowed down and leant towards Bill, who backed away a little from the Scotch mist that accompanied him.

'See, I don't go much on these academic types,' said Royle, now definitely attempting confidentiality. 'Not really my line of country at all. You may not have noticed, but some of the time I don't have a clue what they're talking about.'

'No? Really?' said Bill.

' 'Strue,' said Royle. 'Now, I thought – you being a wide-awake young blade, you might be able to do a bit of ferreting round about things where I'd be at a bit of a loss. People's backgrounds, like, possible motives, that kind of thing. They'd all talk to you, you see, and you'd understand.'

'You obviously don't know university departments if you think we all talk to each other,' said Bill. 'Some of us go for months without. Still, I'm beginning to get your drift.'

'Then again,' said Royle, 'you've been to Oxford College, if I remember, and you might have a few contacts there that could be of help. They might be able to run down a few facts, either about the poor old bugger who died or about some of those other academics who've been to Oxford in their time.'

Bill Bascomb paused for a bit.

'So what it boils down to is, you'd like me to do a bit of detective work – more or less commissioned by you.'

'That's about it,' said Royle. 'I'm looking for a bit of promotion from this little job, so I'll make it worth your while. But God help me if I don't catch anyone.'

Bill Bascomb was exceedingly pleased. Such a suggestion appealed strongly to the 'Adventurous Five' side of his nature. Until not so very long ago Enid Blyton had been his favourite reading. Again, the thought of finding one of his colleagues out to be a brutal murderer was not without its attractions. Quite apart from the fillip it would give to the rather dull life he lead in this dreary little Australian town, he had one or two scruffy Oxford friends who would be glad of an academic job in Australia, and while they would not be very good acquisitions to the department, nor would Dr Day or Dr Porter be any great loss. He had settled on those two already in his mind as the most likely, since he thought the latter had the necessary malice, and the former (when sober, a large qualification) the necessary intelligence to get away with murder – at least when up against the Australian police force. Then again, though he didn't really think that Professor Wickham had either the brains or the guts to do it, the thought of Lucy Wickham weeping copious tears down the bosom of her useful little black dress had a certain dramatic appeal. It would be worth being proved wrong just to see it.

'You're on,' he said.

'Right,' said Royle, foreseeing his load lightened and feeling considerably relieved. 'First of all, then, you've got to be very discreet. Obviously no one must suspect you're in cahoots with us.'

'Right you are,' said Bill.

'And be discreet if you come to see me at the station, because I don't want anyone there to know either.'

'Right you are,' said Bill.

'And not a word to anyone. No taking of people quietly into your confidence because you don't think they did it. Anyone could have done it – anyone at all. Understand?'

'Of course, naturally,' said Bill.

'Good luck, then,' said Royle, awkwardly, extending his hand like a sales manager sending out a raw recruit to take over his first area. Bill Bascomb took it equally awkwardly, and was let out of the police car just outside his block of Menzies College.

He lugged his sherry flagons up to his room, poured himself half a tumblerful, and got on the phone to tell Alice O'Brien about it.

CHAPTER ELEVEN

The Drummondale School

Inspector Royle drove through the gates of the Drummondale School, and through the extensive grounds and playing-fields towards the main school building, a solid Edwardian affair over which John Betjeman had also once cast an eye of over-Catholic appreciation. Clearly, if the New South Wales upper-middle-classes believed in locking up their daughters, they were content with a very open prison for their sons. The gates were wide, the grounds unpatrolled, the general atmosphere was relaxed, not to say soporific. Over on the playing fields a few flannelled fools were putting in a spot of practice, immaculate in their flannels and probably in their foolishness. Otherwise there was little noise to be heard except for an uproar from a distant class-room – no doubt one of the teachers newly recruited from England. They were said to raise the tone, but they did very little for the discipline.

Inspector Royle took all this in approvingly. Here he was on home ground. The Methodist Ladies never came through his hands (to use a not inappropriate metaphor) during term time because they were never allowed outside the walls to get up to anything. But the Drummondale School he had visited frequently in connection with petty pilfering from shops, stolen cars and such like. And then there had been that incendiary lad last year. In most cases it had been discovered that everyone – especially the boys' parents – had been anxious to avoid a prosecution, and Royle counted these as among his most rewarding cases. The general feeling of well-being increased as he got out of the car in front of the moderately imposing front entrance: a passing secretary recognized him immediately, paid due attention to his status and appeared blushingly conscious of the handsome figure he made in his uniform; she ushered him straight in to Mr Doncaster, who she said had been expecting him, and had kept himself as free from engagements as possible. This is something like, thought Royle. This is showing respect for the law.

Mr Doncaster had two very effective manners which had secured and advanced his position in the shifting, volatile world of the Australian private school. One was his parent-pleasing manner, the other was his teacher-to-teacher manner. He could, like an experienced cocktail-mixer, occasionally produce a subtly different blend of the two, and this he now did for Inspector Royle. The latter sank into a very easy easy-chair, feeling at home, respected, and at peace with the world; except, of course, for the damned investigation. He felt more like bemoaning his lot than asking questions, and he let Doncaster talk on as his eye roamed the study with a renewed interest which came from the fact that this was the first time he had been there on a case in which Doncaster could be considered in the light of a suspect. It was a gentleman-scholar's room: photographs of cricket teams, school groups, a smart army photograph with a rather artificially grim expression. On the wall a college shield, and a cricket bat signed by one of the school's dimmest past students, who had gone on to play for the state and become a Country Party politician. The bookshelves were full of books, old, dirty, and looking very thumbed. Royle idly wondered whether the thumbs that had thumbed them had been Doncaster's thumbs, or if they had been picked up cheap in a second-hand bookshop. He'd never actually seen Doncaster reading, and unless he actually saw people reading, Royle was inclined to suspect that they never did, since he had no time whatsoever for the occupation himself.

Mr Doncaster was commenting on the terrible nature of the atrocity, and how things struck him:

'Quite apart from the shock one feels oneself,' he said (he could be relied on to wield a magisterial 'one'), 'and it really *is* a shock when one remembers one was talking to the poor old fellow only a matter of hours before, there is the damage to the community as a whole. One of our most important assets is that we are quiet, rural – a bit withdrawn from the fuss of twentieth-century life, as you might say. That's why quite a few parents in Sydney, *quite* a few, prefer to send their boys to – to a place like this. Anything of this kind is bound to disturb our "image", to use the current term. That's why it is so important to get the thing out of the way as soon as possible. I'm speaking here as a professional man, of course, but also as an ordinary citizen of Drummondale. Stop all the talk, get rid of the nasty atmosphere, so we can get back to normal, that's my view.'

Mr Doncaster was inclined to say everything twice over, even if what he said was usually straightforward enough to be grasped first time. One of his staff after a speech-day had said his address had reminded him of Mr Chadband, and he had received a dignified word of thanks and a degree of modest advancement as a result.

'Don't you agree?' added Doncaster, as his last words echoed to silence.

'Oh yes, quite, quite,' said Royle, who hadn't been listening. 'And then there's my career to think about.'

Mr Doncaster's expression of sympathetic interest was in his most sincere and encouraging vein. Royle

112

pulled himself back from entering into his personal problems, and tried to focus his mind on what he was supposed to be there for.

'You say you were talking to the old chappie,' he said. 'Could you tell me what you were talking about at the Wickhams' party?'

'Yes, of course. I've been doing my best to remember, knowing that you would be interested. Of course, you have to remember it *was* a party, and one can't always remember details afterwards.'

Royle nodded agreement and tried to look interested. He took out his cigarettes, and before he could fumble for his match Mr Doncaster was behind his chair, lighting his Pall Mall with the unobtrusive air of a good waiter.

'Well, then,' he said as he sat down behind his desk, and spread his hands, palms down, over its paper-bestrewn surface, 'we talked about the school, of course. I suppose they have to show interest in the local institutions as they're travelling around – but actually I think it was Mrs Lullham who introduced the subject. Not that her son is to be counted as one of our major successes, I'm afraid –' here he gave a conspiratorial smile at Inspector Royle, who knew perfectly well why – 'Still, she is grateful, and I must say the graziers in general *are* very proud of the school, and we are greatly indebted to them – in every way. So of course it's pleasing when they do praise us to outsiders. Yes, then; what else? Oh yes – we talked a little about the curriculum, sports, outside activities, scouting – that sort of thing.'

'And is that all?' asked Royle to gain time, not seeing anything to latch on to here.

'I'm afraid it is. Certainly all I can remember. We all sort of moved around you know, as one does, so I was only talking to him for a comparatively small part of the evening.'

'Was there anything you talked about that he seemed more interested in than other things you talked about?' asked Royle, his questions getting rather desperate as he found Mr Doncaster increasingly soporific.

'Not that I remember, no,' said Doncaster after a pause for mature thought. 'What exactly had you in mind, Inspector?'

The only thing that was remotely on his mind was something he would rather have phrased delicately, but, the question being sprung at him like that, he utterly failed to do so.

'You don't think he could have had a thing about Boy Scouts, do you? I don't have to tell you about scout-masters and the like. Do you think he could have been some kind of sexual pervert?'

He brought out the last phrase with considerable aplomb, and gazed up at Doncaster's handsome, aquiline face which did not betray the shadow of a smile. Doncaster had long practice at keeping a straight face when little boys said silly things, and – like most good schoolmasters – he didn't have any sense of humour to speak of anyway. He put his fingers together in a judicious, weighing-the-evidence kind of way:

'Oh, I don't think so, Inspector. No, I didn't get any feeling of that. And, of course, he would be well past it, even if he had once had that . . . interest, shall we say.'

'Some people never get past it,' said Royle optimistically.

'And, you know, when I said he didn't show special interest in any one part of the conversation, I should perhaps have added that he really didn't show much interest in anything at all. He was just making conversation, more or less automatically. He seemed to me terribly old and tired – one felt almost sorry for him, felt he must have undertaken something well beyond his strength.' Mr Doncaster's loquacity paused as he tried to find a way of summing it up. 'Most of the evening he sort of flickered, you know, as if he was about to go out.'

'He's certainly snuffed it now, anyway,' said Royle coarsely. Mr Doncaster, after a fraction of a second for consideration, allowed himself the luxury of a man-to-man laugh, though he carefully kept any suggestion of coarseness out of it.

'You didn't see anything in his behaviour to the other guests that was in any way unusual, did you?' asked Royle, wiping his mouth on his handkerchief, and fingering the sweaty arm-pits of his shirt.

'Nothing, really; nothing at all. There *was* the little episode at the end of the evening – the one involving Professor Wickham. No doubt you have already been told about that?'

What had the Wickhams done to people that every one of their guests should remember this so clearly, and bring it up? Never had hospitality received such ill returns. Royle indicated that he had had several accounts of the episode already.

'What did you make of it, sir?' he asked.

Mr Doncaster deprecated the 'sir' with an elegant, almost Italianate gesture of the hands.

'Personally, I wouldn't make too much of it. I doubt whether it had any importance. I'm not trying to teach you your job, of course, but I think on the whole that the incident only stands out because – well, frankly, it hadn't been a particularly bright evening all in all, and so no one noticed this, and in a way welcomed it.'

'You don't think there could have been any hostility between the two from way back, then?'

'That I can't say, of course. But I don't remember anyone suggesting that they had met before – correct me if I'm wrong. And you know these old men *do* get a little cantankerous at times, especially when their comfort isn't being attended to.' He quickly amended this: 'When they imagine that their comfort is not being attended to.' He had remembered that the Wickhams were, after all, parents. 'It's not *all* that easy to keep people of that age happy. Personally I wouldn't pay overmuch attention to the matter – just a trivial incident.'

Royle had noticed, however, that he had thought it worth talking about at some length.

'You yourself were at Oxford, I believe,' he said, conversationally. He had found out after struggling through the school prospectus that Mr Doncaster was MA (Oxon), and had ascertained by telephoning the librarian at police headquarters in Sydney that this meant he had obtained his degree at Oxford. He had later confirmed this with Bill Bascomb, not trusting librarians.

'That's true,' said Doncaster.

'Did you know the old chap there then?' asked Royle.

'No, I'm afraid our paths never crossed.'

Doncaster wasn't being very forthcoming, but Royle decided that with an old and valued client like him he could afford for once to betray his ignorance.

'Can you tell me one thing?' he asked with an air of exasperation. 'Practically everyone around here seems to have been to Oxford College, and yet not a soul seems to have clapped eyes on Belville-Smith while they were there. Seems bloody unlikely, if you'll pardon my saying so. Unless he was some kind of hermit.'

Mr Doncaster put on his kindest air, the one he used while attempting to explain the Wars of the Roses to the more backward classes, and tried to look as if he thought Royle's ignorance was not just natural but even in some way commendable.

'I see it must be confusing for you,' he said, and went smoothly into a detailed account of the size of Oxford University, the large number of different colleges that made up the University, the independence of those same

116

colleges, the organization of the tutorial system, and several other related points. He was so experienced at exposition of this kind – unlike Bill Bascomb, who always assumed that anything he knew was something any idiot ought to know – that Royle seemed to be taking some of it in.

'I get you,' he said at the end. 'So if you weren't in the same college as he was, the chances are you wouldn't clap eyes on him.'

'Exactly,' said Doncaster.

'Even if you were studying English.'

'Even so. Though you might attend some of his lectures in that case, that is if he gave any.'

'None of that lot out there did, or so they say.'

'Well, of course, they *could* be telling the truth,' said Mr Doncaster. 'People go to fewer lectures there than they would here. And I must say my impression was that he was not the most cogent or inspiring of speakers – whatever he may have been in his younger days.'

'And you weren't studying English . . .' said Royle.

'History,' said Doncaster.

'And you weren't in his college?'

'That's right, I was at St Catherine's.'

Doncaster noticed that – as with most Australians – saying 'St Catherine's' meant no more than if he had said 'St John's' or 'St Edmund Hall'. All equally conjured up a picture of lawned quadrangles, jovial porters and ivy-cluttered walls. Except, of course, that for Royle, judged by his face, no image was conjured up at all. He might just as well have said 'St Francis of Assisi's'.

'When were you studying at Uni?' asked Royle, beginning to make I-might-as-well-be-getting-along motions in his chair.

'Just before the war,' said Doncaster. 'I was lucky, I got my study in before I did my bit. Oxford wasn't quite the same afterwards, I'm told, with all those ex-servicemen around.'

117

'Ex-servicemen?' said Royle, incredulously. 'You mean people actually came out of the forces and went up to Uni?'

'Yes indeed. And it made things enormously crowded there. Most of the lectures were full, and libraries too. It wasn't like that in pre-war days. I suppose it has gone back to normal now. I certainly hope so.'

'I bet it's not like in your day,' said Royle, edging forward in his seat. 'Lots of bloody long-haired layabouts if the lot we get here is anything to go on. Wasn't Professor Wickham there after the war, by the by − about 1947 or 1948? He said something about ex-servicemen, I recall, though I didn't get his point at the time.'

'I believe he was, but I've never discussed Oxford with him. He's younger than I so, I doubt if he can have been there in my time. And of course I had no thought of coming to Australia at that stage, so I didn't go out of my way to mix with the Australian groups there.'

Royle thought he detected a note of pommie-bastardy there, but he let it pass.

'I believe his wife followed him to Oxford later, didn't she?'

'I believe so. As I say, I was not there myself, but I *do* seem to remember some talk about her from friends. You know the sort of story that goes round . . .'

'I do,' said Royle emphatically, getting interested at last. 'That's something that could be important. What kind of talk was this?'

'No, it wouldn't be fair to say anything, Inspector. After all, the memory is very vague, it was entirely second-hand, and it could have been a quite different girl. Perhaps I shouldn't have said anything at all.'

Royle felt like telling him to give him the story, whatever girl it was about, but he left the subject regretfully.

'Now, after the party, sir, you came back here, I suppose?'

'Yes, indeed; I left immediately after the Professor, and I suppose I'd be back here five minutes later.'

'Is there anyone who can testify to that?'

'I'm afraid not, Inspector. You'll just have to take my word.' He gave Royle a straight, piercing look which was meant to convince him that a schoolmaster's word was as good as a parson's any day. Royle had his own opinion of schoolmasters, however. And of parsons.

'It would help if anyone saw you arrive home,' he said. 'You don't have a gate-keeper, for instance.'

'Alas, no. I let myself in. We do have a night porter, but I'm quite sure he didn't see me. He is inclined to doze. I believe he is a postman in the daylight hours — he's saving up for his passage home, poor man.'

'And you live alone, do you, like Miss Tambly?'

'*Not* like Miss Tambly,' said Doncaster, 'but, yes, I am a bachelor, if that's what you mean, Inspector.'

'Well,' said Royle, 'I think that will probably be all — at least for the moment, sir,' and he heaved his bulk into the air. A moment later he wished he hadn't.

'Have a small drink, Inspector,' said Mr Doncaster as he usually did after his interviews with the police. He waited till they were over so there could be no question of corrupting the force. His scruples were quite lost on Inspector Royle, who merely cursed him mentally for not asking before he had made the effort of getting himself up. The thought crossed his mind that not one of the academics had offered him a drop, though he was pretty sure most of them kept stacks of it in their rooms and he'd actually seen yards of it in Alice O'Brien's. He thanked his God for the Australian private schools.

'Just a quick one, then,' he said.

When he got back to the station, in moderately mellow mood, Royle put through a call to Bill Bascomb at

Menzies College. It was just before lunch time, so he knew he would find him at home.

'Anything your end?' he asked.

'Give us a chance, Inspector,' said Bill. 'I've only been on it a few hours. I'm not used to the game.'

'Have you had any ideas about how to set about it, then?'

'Well, I've sent a telegram to a friend at Oxford. He's working on the *Oxford Mail* – that's the local paper – and I thought he might be able to look in his files for anything interesting about the people who were up there – Wickham and the rest.'

'Criminal things, you mean?'

'Well, not necessarily. I presume you'll have been in touch with the Oxford police over that.' (Bloody young twit, trying to teach me my job, thought Royle. He hadn't.) 'It just occurred to me that there might be something not criminal, but which would give us a link between Belville-Smith and someone here. College gossip, some old scandal or other. Then we could follow it up – you know, try to trip them up, or accuse them of covering up and get them confused.'

'Good idea,' said Royle heartily. 'None of them will admit to having set eyes on him before, so if we get a lead like that we might be able to twist the knife a bit.'

'Exactly,' said Bill, sounding as if he didn't quite like the image. 'Then I'm going to try a bit of probing at coffee-time tomorrow.'

'OK,' said Royle, 'but don't make it too obvious. The last thing we want is for anyone to think you're in this with me.'

'I'll be as crafty as I know how,' said Bill, 'but I don't think anyone will twig. After all, we're pretty unlikely bedfellows.'

'Too bloody right,' said Inspector Royle.

CHAPTER TWELVE

The English Department

When he arrived at work the next morning, at his usual time of ten to ten-thirty, Bill Bascomb was surprised by the look of vindictive hatred which he received from Professor Wickham as they passed in the corridor. It was a why-do-I-engage-these-Oxford-adolescents look and it boded little good for Bill's future. Deciding that extreme measures were warranted by his new status as Watson to Royle's Sherlock (or possibly vice versa) he did what he would have done in any case — listened outside the Professor's door. Owing to the 'temporary', jerry-built nature of the sprawling hut in which the English Department was accommodated, he soon found out the cause of his unpopularity.

'Do you know what that fool Bascomb has done?' Professor Wickham nearly shouted down the phone, for once forgetting to address his wife with his usual wheedling ceremoniousness. 'He's sent a telegram to some idiot friend at Oxford, someone on the *Mail*, asking him for anything he could dig up on any of the Oxford people around here. I've never heard of such bloody cheek.'

There was a long pause. Clearly Lucy had never heard of such bloody cheek either. It was one of those rare occasions on which they were completely at one. The

121

honeymoon period between Mrs Wickham and the latest young recruit from Oxford was obviously destined to be even shorter than usual.

'Me, and Day, and Doncaster,' went on Wickham. 'But he's also put the other names in, just in case. Except the O'Brien, of course . . . Well, they're in this together, that's obvious − some childish nonsense they've thought up . . . No, I couldn't get the thing suppressed. It's already sent. Wylie the post-master up here said it was more than his job was worth, but he thought I ought to know . . . Yes, of course I gave him something . . . How could it be much when I never have much?'

Bill Bascomb went busily into the secretary's office as someone came along the corridor. Coming out a minute later with some unnecessary stationery, he heard Wickham say: 'I don't see how he could be on to that. There was never anything in the papers. It's just black ingratitude, and that's what really gets me: you give a chap a job, only just down, nothing in writing except this supposed article which will never see the light of day I'm willing to bet, and when you expect an ounce of loyalty, this is your reward . . . I imagine it's just some childish itch to play detective . . . Why I let him go on to the permanent staff I'll never know. I must have been off my head.'

Bill shifted uneasily from one foot to the other. He was mentally kicking himself for sending the cable off from the University Post Office − but then who could have imagined it would have been shown to his boss? In civilized countries telegrams were a private matter, like one's prayers or one's bank balance. Here, obviously, it was different altogether. Here it was the done thing to go around blabbing people's telegrams over the entire campus.

'What? The Inspector?' Wickham's voice boomed throught the processed cardboard partition. 'Inspector Royle? Why should he be coming to talk to you? I told him all that we could give him – there's nothing you could add. Yes, I suppose he has to, as routine, still . . . All right, I'll ring you back later. Be nice to him.'

Bill took himself off as the receiver was bashed down on to its holder. Whichever way you regarded it, this was a set-back to his investigations. Here was one suspect who obviously wasn't going to be unburdening his soul to him in an unguarded moment. In fact it looked at the moment as if he wasn't going to be talking to him for the rest of the term. He would have to pin his hopes on the rest of the staff, at least until he heard something from Oxford. Perhaps he and Alice would be able to pick something up during the coffee break.

Alice's reception of the news of his new position as side-kick to the unimpressive Inspector Royle had been less than flattering. She had let out an eldritch shriek of laughter, and had run through a collection of fictional characters – Watson, Bunter, Lugg and Fox – which was designed to suggest that as a detective combination she didn't find him and Royle very impressive. She was inclined, too, to be snooty about his being in the clear, and was taking some pleasure in herself still being a suspect. Nor had she been very hopeful about picking up anything by pumping the other members of the department, trying to catch them in an unguarded moment.

'It's not as though the art of conversation is being revived in this remote spot,' she said. 'I've never noticed any eighteenth-century expansiveness.'

'I agree some of them will be difficult,' Bill had replied. 'Merv Raines, for instance. The Porter won't be any walkover either – she still confines herself to words of two syllables when she's talking to me.'

'Have you got that far?' said Alice. 'She must have her eyes on you, unlikely as that may seem.'

'But the others talk enough – and even Raines can

do when he's got a few beers in him. In the end they're bound to let something slip that gives the game away.'

'The precept of Miss Marple, if I remember rightly,' said Alice. 'Watch it, or your own precious little throat may be in for a shave. They always do it a second time, according to Aunt Agatha.'

'I did lock my door last night, I must admit,' said Bill.

'So did old Belville-Smith on the night in question, I expect,' said Alice cosily.

'Anyway, we Fearless Five never worry about our own throats,' said Bill. 'Give up the pouring-cold-water lark. There's got to be something somewhere, and the likelihood is it's among the academics. Whichever way you look at it, some guilty secret shared between Belville-Smith and the Turbervilles is a non-starter. Someone's got something to hide, and it's pretty sure to be one of us.'

'I've no doubts about that, believe me. If I shuffle around in the Porter's private life of her academic career I'd be disappointed if I couldn't fetch up something pretty murky. But how is that going to help? There can't be anything to connect her with that poor old goat, and we're just going to land up with a lot of useless dirt.'

'Since when have you despised useless dirt?' asked Bill.

'Fair enough,' said Alice. 'All right, I'll give it a go.'

So when the department gathered for coffee – minus Professor Wickham who always absented himself when he could not look on his staff with the eye of favour – Bill and Alice turned the talk to the murder, and kept it there. It didn't need much turning or keeping. The talk for the last few days had been of very little else. At first the members of the department who had not been at the Wickhams' gathering had been rather unpleasantly self-congratulatory about it. Smithson, the only other remaining young Oxonian, had been at Bathurst, conducting a weekend school for external students, and his presence there throughout the night in question had been vouched for by two very willing young externals. The other two absentees had been the two tutors, who had apparently been deemed too junior, or perhaps too crude, to be invited. The slight had given them one of their rare, brief, us-against-the-rest moods, which were a relief from the us-against-each-other ones. By now they were beginning to get bored by the whole thing, and to wish they had had a part in an event which was obviously destined to be the major topic of conversation in Drummondale for the next couple of years. Their presence would also have given them immense cachet in the poky little country towns from which they came. The consolation was that, if there was a certain glamour about being a suspect, there was also a certain danger, particularly in Australia. Though the police force of Drummondale was probably no more stupid and vicious than the police forces of any other small town, one still needed more than innocence to protect oneself. So Spokes and Finlay sat around only vaguely listening to the conversation, mentally rearranging their card-indexes and being congratulated by Professor Wickham on their method.

'Did you ever read any of the old boy's stuff?' said Bill Bascomb to Dr Porter.

'Never.'

'Not even when you knew he was coming?'

'Never in my vocabulary means on no occasion,' said Dr Porter, with a smile to freeze the Pacific.

'Sorry,' said Bill, ingratiatingly. 'I just thought it was your area — Wickham said something about the eighteenth century when he was introducing him, didn't he?'

'The eighteenth century,' said Dr Porter through her tight lips, 'is a considerable area of study.'

'What *had* he written on, do you know?' asked Alice.

'I have no idea, I'm afraid,' said Dr Porter. 'Certainly not on Akenside.'

Akenside was the subject of Dr Porter's thesis, a poet so utterly minor, so totally lacking in any spark of originality or fire, that he had been well within the scope of her mind. The thesis had been virtually unexamined, since nobody in Australia could be found willing to waste their time reading the outpourings of her subject. However her footnoting and her bibliography had been found to conform in an exemplary fashion to the commandments of the MLA style-sheet, and she had been granted her doctorate like many another, through a sort of academic exhaustion. She drank her coffee in moderate, regular sips, with the air of one who did not let a little thing like murder upset her academic routine, unlike other more volatile souls. Bill gave her one more look, and turned toward Merv Raines, who was sprawled over two chairs, a heavy, ugly grey pullover adding to his ungainliness, glowering into his coffee cup, and mentally cosseting the chip on his shoulder.

'The old boy didn't do anything in your line, anyway,' said Bill, 'not to judge from what you were saying at the party.'

'That's for sure,' said Merv.

'You said he wasn't well up in Australian literature at all, didn't you?' said Bill. Merv unbuttoned the corner of his mouth a little further, remembering his grievance.

'He didn't say much, but I guessed. I don't think he'd even heard of Henry Handel Richardson. I had to give him, like, a bit of a resumé of *Richard Mahoney*. And I bet if I'd er gone on to Lawson, Clarke and Judith Wright it'd er been the same.'

'I should think it would,' said Bill, conscious that a year ago he hadn't heard of them either.

'Bloody condescending bastards,' said Merv.

'Perhaps Merv did him in as part of the fight against colonialist condescension,' said Alice. 'An ideological murder. They're pretty fashionable these days.'

'Don't be bloody daft,' said Merv, swilling down the

126

last of his coffee and relapsing into renewed glower.

'The trouble with this murder,' said Bill, 'is that nobody at all has a shadow of a motive. It's not like that in detective stories. Look at Aunt Agatha, for instance. Usually it's some ghastly old bugger gets done in that everyone else in the book would have been only too happy to stick the knife into.'

'That's true,' said Smithson; 'and even then it usually turns out to be the policeman.'

'Yes, that's a fast one,' said Alice. 'I suppose there's no hope that it could be the policeman in this case, is there?'

'You mean Royle in his younger and more idealistic days wanting to go to Oxford like Jude the Obscure, and getting the cool brush-off from Belville-Smith?'

'The mind boggles,' said Alice. 'Anyone less like Jude the Obscure than Inspector Royle I cannot imagine.'

Dr Day was getting rather restive.

'I'm bored with this whole business,' he said. 'Quite apart from anything else, I can't remember a damned thing about what happened the whole night. It's the only time in my whole life I wish I'd been less drunk than I was.'

'Doesn't it frighten you, that?' asked Bill. 'It would me. I think I'd get nightmares thinking what I might have done while I was under the influence.'

'I've been under the influence practically continuously since I was thirty, and for quite a bit of the time before that,' said Day. 'I've done a lot of funny things in my time, but murder isn't one of them, so I'm pretty sure I didn't take the carving knife and hare off in the direction of the Yarumba Motel. When you've been drunk so often you know the sort of things you do and the sort of things you don't do.'

'I suppose you would learn by experience?' said Alice.

'Anyone going to the smorgasbord lunch?' asked Day, without any particular air of wishing to change the subject.

127

'You without a doubt,' said Bill.

The smorgasbord lunch was a weekly affair at the students' union – but only for the staff, or course. You could eat and drink as much as you liked for a dollar, so it attracted all those who couldn't resist an apparent bargain. Various unappetizing messes of a peculiarly unScandinavian nature were provided, and you could drink limitless glasses of tuppenny headache wine. It was not the food that attracted Dr Day.

'Course I'm going,' he said. 'Never missed one yet. I've got a tutorial at two. You've no idea how much better they go since they started these lunches.'

'Actually, we had heard rumours of how they were going,' said Alice, who believed in keeping sober until the approaching horrors of high table made a few glasses inevitable.

'I find it releases the mind,' said Peter Day, with his cunning, self-depreciating little smile. 'One can range more widely. It's a liberal education for these students. After all, they don't meet a really well-travelled man every day.'

'Do you ever actually talk about the topic you're supposed to be dealing with?' asked Dr Porter.

'How should I know? I never remember a thing about them. Anyway, how would I know what we were supposed to be talking about?'

'It is posted up on the departmental notice-board,' Dr Porter pointed out.

'What departmental notice-board?' asked Dr Day, hearing of it for the first time.

'So it's a bit of a lucky dip, coming to your tutorials, is it?' asked Alice.

'Well, what they need, I think, is to see the book in a wider context. Anyone can talk about a book, after all. And they have read the thing themselves. What I give them is the wider context.'

'Along with sexual reminiscences, analyses of Spanish

politics in the thirties, accounts of your travels with a donkey on three continents, etcetera, etcetera, etcetera, I believe,' said Alice.

'Really?' said Peter Day, genuinely interested. 'Is that what we've been talking about? You see what I mean, then, about a liberal education. It must have opened their eyes immensely. It's the sort of thing you never get in Australian schools.'

Bill was somewhat depressed by the results of his first little efforts at drawing his colleagues out. He had the impression that even if he had been able to get everything down on tape and play it over and over to himself later, he would get very little out of it except a stupendous boredom. If one of his colleagues had something to hide, the general level of conversation gave them plenty of trivia to hide it under.

He decided to pocket his principles and partake of the smorgasbord lunch. He had only done so once, and had been very publicly sick afterwards, so he was rather reluctant, but there was no knowing what Day might not reveal when drunk. True his mind usually travelled along drearily predictable lines at such times, but if he had done the murder, the reason might be lying fairly close to the top of his jumbled mind, and there might be some chance of it emerging as the alcohol level rose. The only question was, whether he would be able to recognize it and disentangle it from the rest.

So, at half past twelve he trudged up the hill to the union, observing Dr Day's car parked at an impossible angle just by the union door (the walk was only one of a minute and a half, but Day had been affected by the general Australian desire to be the first nation to be born without such useless members as legs). Clearly Day had, as usual, managed to get in at opening time.

Bill walked disconsolately along the trestle table along which the Australo-Scandaniavian delicacies were ranged. There was a large stewing-saucepan full of bits

129

of pork sausage and tinned peas. There was another labelled 'Spaghetti Neapolitan', full of brilliant red and white goo, rather like gory entrails in a Hammer film. There were cold mutton chops with baked beans poured over them. As an enterprise, this was not calculated to persuade the Australians that the Swedes were on to a good thing. Luckily there were no Swedes present to protest against the aspersion on their national palate. Bill spied a pyramid of plates containing some rather wilted ham salads. He took one, and looked around for Peter Day. As he expected, Peter had bagged a seat in the corner where the flagons of red and white wine were – making sure they were within easy reach of his right hand. The warden of the union was looking at him in disgust, wondering whether there ought to be a change in the regulations for these affairs. Others less involved financially were simply avoiding him.

'Thought I'd try it again today,' said Bill apologetically. 'Chef doesn't seem to have got any new ideas.'

'Oh, are you eating?' asked Peter.

'I thought it was the idea.'

'The secret,' said Peter, 'is not to start until after you've had three glasses.' He waved his large tumbler. 'Then you don't notice the food.'

'I suppose you wouldn't,' said Bill.

'This is my third now,' said Peter, draining off half a tumbler. 'Keep my place. Everyone wants to get near the grog.' And he weaved off towards the table, as usual looking like a music-hall comic doing a parody of a drunk asked to walk a white line. He returned in the same fashion, carrying a plate piled high with a bit of everything, and spilling gravy and little bits of spaghetti over himself as he went. As he sat down he reached straight for one of the flagons and tucked into both food and drink with appetite.

'People make a fuss about their food,' he said, 'but I find that most things go down.'

'As far as these dos are concerned I find that most things come up,' said Bill.

Peter Day laughed, and a little more gravy spilled over his trousers.

'Did I ever tell you about the girl from Sheffield I met at my adult education classes?' he asked.

'Yes,' said Bill, 'innumerable times. So often that the story is engraved word for word on my memory like the Lord's Prayer. So often that I wake up in the morning muttering it by rote.' It was as well to exaggerate a little with Peter Day when he was drunk, since he was inclined not to take no for an answer. 'Don't you have any reminiscences drawn from any other period of your life?'

Peter took the invitation perfectly seriously, thought a little, then launched into a story about a brothel in Khartoum, which somehow became a brothel on the left bank in Paris about half-way through. This in turn gave way, without any obvious transition, to a story about illicit love in Argentina in the days of Eva Peron. By this time Peter Day had had seven tumblers, had got rid of his plateful partly down his mouth and partly over his person, and was beginning to show signs of wear.

'Must have been a change after Oxford,' said Bill, desperate for a change of subject, quite apart from his supposed investigations. Peter Day's eyes refocused, as if trying to remember what or where Oxford was. Finally some sort of light seemed to strike.

'Paris was before Oxford,' he said firmly. 'Canada was after, and Khartoum was after, but Paris was before. Went to Ox . . . Oxford late, you know. Not like you young sprigs of the aristocracy.'

Bill accepted the implied insult, though it was untrue.

'What exactly were you doing at Oxford?' he asked.

'Research,' said Peter, very definitely. Then he made another attempt to focus his eyes, on what Bill was not quite sure. 'Research into the poetry of George Eliot. Or the plays of Dickens. Or was it the novels of Mrs Humphry Ward? I've forgotten which. Done 'em all in my time. I'll say this, I've never wanted for a good subject. They ought to send the honours students to me for ideas.'

'Weren't you working at the same time?' asked Bill.

'Worked at the Bodle . . . Bodleian for a bit,' said Peter, not noticeably reluctant to tell. 'In the background, you know. In the . . . background. Getting the books up for the readers. Bit of cata . . . cataloguing too. That sort of thing.'

He was finding it increasingly difficult to concentrate. He had something else on his mind, and his eyes kept straying round to the flagons, and jealously fixing a look of hatred on anyone who came near them. On one occasion they had run out, and he was going to make sure that this time they ran out into his glass.

'Was it interesting?' asked Bill.

'Eh? Was what interesting?'

'Working. In. The Bodleian.'

'If you liked books, I suppose,' said Peter, as if trying to be fair. 'I didn't go much on it myself.'

'Pleasant company, though.'

'If you call librarians pleasant company, you must have some kind of a . . . some kind of a – ' Peter searched at his leisure for a word, and finally found one – : 'some kind of a kink.'

'Still, it must have brought you into contact with all the academics,' said Bill.

'Best adacemics never went near the Bodleian,' said Peter firmly. 'Same everywhere. Good academic should b'able to go to the lecture hall and talk for an hour on any subject under the sun. If he can't, he's wasting his time.'

'And if he does, he's wasting the students' time,' said Bill, but he wasn't being listened to.

'Anyway, I'm glad to say I can, and I do.'

Bill knew he did, and he also knew he shouldn't. He switched the subject back again.

'So you didn't meet Lord David or any of those?'

'Christ no. Anyway I was down in the slacks . . . down in the . . . *stacks*. Didn't meet anyone. Not a soul. Not the ghost of a soul. Not the ghost of a . . . ghost.' His voice was getting far away, as if he was talking of a long time ago. 'Only the odd little librarian lass, burrowing away there . . . burrowing away there, like a little . . . mole . . . a little, snuffling . . . mole. Get me another drink, will you, Bill? I don't think I could lift the bloody flagon. And you've got to get your money's worth.'

Bill got him another drink, and then half-walked, half-carried him over to the fresh air. He was already ten minutes late for his tutorial. Quite suddenly, as the heavy afternoon sun revived him, he shook off Bill's protective arm, and shot off determinedly down the hill, only to trip over a small hillock in the grass. Half an hour later Bill saw him through the window holding forth, and he thought he heard the name Mintinguette. He could not see if there were any students in his room, but he rather suspected not. At least that was one tradition he had picked up at Oxford.

When Professor Wickham came down to the department from his sandwich and coffee lunch, he rang his wife to see how the interview with Inspector Royle had gone.

'All right. Quite all right,' said Lucy in a rather surprised manner. 'He was very nice. I'll tell you this evening. I'm busy now. I've got something on the stove.'

Professor Wickham was puzzled, because he thought he could hear heavy breathing behind her voice.

CHAPTER THIRTEEN

Women of Property

As Royle drove from the Wickhams' residence towards the outskirts of town, and thence on to the gravel road which led to the Lullham property, he had a secret source of self-congratulation which had nothing to do with the progress of the case. Several times he came near to smiling, and frequently he passed his tongue around his lips, as if he had been eating ice-cream. This secret source, and preparing his approach to Peggy Lullham, kept him pretty happy throughout most of the long, bumpy drive out to Tara Magna. He had two different manners with the grazing aristocracy: for the most part he was servile, as befitted his dependent station, but when he had recently conferred favours, he adopted that hearty benevolent-paternal manner which is one of the law's best cards. Sometimes this manner could wear a little thin, and a distinct trace of his natural bully-boy manner show through, it is true, but in this he differed in no way from most benevolent paternalists, and he did try to keep it in check. After all, these were people with money.

The landscape became drier, dustier, more choking the farther he went. The Lullham property seemed to be in no condition to resist the rigours of the drought. A knot of cattle-men and jackaroos gathered by a cross-

roads looked as if they could do with a cold Grafton's.
The paddocks looked the same way, but they wouldn't
be getting one. Royle drove up to the Lullham residence,
a long, low, much-built-on-to old house, which looked
comfortable and homely. The front door stood open,
and as he got out of his car he was conscious of a curtain
falling back into place at one of the downstairs
windows. He thought to himself with some satisfaction
that he must have been waited for for some time.

Mrs Lullham came hesitantly towards the open front
door as he walked up to it, and he could tell by the
nervous flutter of her hands that she was expecting an
ordeal of the most ferocious kind. Her hair looked as
if it was used to weekly attention from someone expensive, but hadn't had it very recently – it looked dead
and perfunctorily brushed, and the woman's skin
looked tired, the make-up carelessly applied. Royle
didn't feel anything that could be identified as pity, but
he did get a certain satisfaction in acting the part of
deliverer from worry and fear. He held up his hand in
a manner which derived largely from his experience
earlier in his career of stopping the traffic in the high
street on Saturday mornings. He had always felt good
doing that.

'Now, before we get under way,' he said in his best
Dock-Green manner, 'let's get this clear. I'm not in the
least interested in that other little matter any longer.'

'Really, Inspector?' said Peggy Lullham hopefully,
experimenting with a little-girl flutter of the eyelashes,
for she had heard of Inspector Royle's reputation.

'Not at all, ma'am,' said Royle, showing disappoint-
ingly little reaction to her advances. 'That's over and
done with as far as I'm concerned, and has nothing to
do with this murder in any case. I haven't been a
policeman all these years without knowing that people
can do some funny things at times' (and profiting from
this fact, he might have added), 'and anyone can see you

must have been off your head with worry about this drought.'

As a matter of fact Peggy Lullham had refurnished the living-room on the drought-relief payments, and her main worry was whether she and her husband would be able to get away for their bi-annual trip to The Old Country next year, but she entered wholeheartedly into Royle's little fiction and breathed a theatrical sigh of relief.

'You're so understanding, Inspector. As you say, it was a case of complete absence of mind, but it's difficult to make someone like John Darcy understand that. The shopkeeper's mind, you know. You must see an awful lot of it. Come in, won't you, Inspector, and I'll try to remember anything that could be of any help.'

She led the way through the hall into the sitting-room, which was large, expensively furnished, but comfortable. As she motioned Royle into one of the large luxurious arm chairs, tailor-made for policemen, she stood by the mantelpiece – a heavy, capable woman who looked as if in the past she would have been able to turn her hand to anything. Now she was running a little to fat, and the remains of a nervous diffidence sat oddly on her, as if she were uncertain of her role. Royle remembered her penchant for shop-lifting pretty, feminine clothes, and began to conjecture whether she wore frilly underwear. On this occasion he was not particularly anxious to be given the chance of finding out.

'Have a beer, Inspector. I've got some on ice,' said Mrs Lullham.

'I'd love one,' said Royle before she had finished. 'I've had a thirsty day, so I'll forget the rule book for once.'

'You won't find me reminding you of it, anyway,' said Mrs Lullham, bustling towards the kitchen.

'I've just got you and Mrs McKay,' said Royle, raising his voice to the bull-bellow he habitually used with his children: 'I say I've only got you and Mrs McKay to go, and then I've had a word with everyone of importance, I think.'

'Nice to be important, of course,' shouted Mrs Lullham from the kitchen, where she was fussing around and putting Royle's glass on a tray of all things, 'but really neither Joan nor I had met the old chap before, so I don't think we'll have much to add that'll be of any use.'

'That's what I guessed,' said Royle, relaxing further into his armchair, which was really almost as comfortable as if it were old, 'but of course one simply has to see everyone in a case like this – the rule book does insist on that. Otherwise you can see now it would appear to the others involved, can't you?'

'Would you like me to ring Joan McKay and get her over here now?' said Peggy Lullham, coming back to the living-room with a dewy glass of the nectar of the Australian Gods. 'She's only on the next property, as you know, so she could be here in half an hour.'

Royle reflected for a moment. It wasn't the right procedure, but then, these two hens weren't going to be able to give him anything. Peggy Lullham had a generous soul and a guilty conscience, whereas Joan McKay was known to be on the near side. The McKays' Scottish ancestry came out in some odd little ways: they took their holidays in the Far East instead of Europe, and pretended an interest in Asiatic culture which wouldn't have deceived a koala bear. With a bit of luck, Royle thought, he'd be well set here for another couple of beers and a pleasant, undemanding chat. He made up his mind.

'OK, that sounds fine, if you would,' he said. 'Tell her I'd be obliged, as a special favour . . .'

Mrs Lullham went into the hall, and Royle heard her say that he was being 'charming', in a voice that was obviously intended to carry back to him. He was being buttered up.

One and a half glasses later Mrs McKay arrived, and Royle took the opportunity of Peggy Lullham's going to let her in to have a really good belch – one of the rafter-ringing variety he entertained his family with on those rare occasions when he stayed at home of an evening. Thus relieved, and feeling several trouser-sizes smaller, he positively sprang to his feet when the ladies came in – he'd seen it done somewhere, though he didn't see the point of it himself – and ushered Joan McKay into a chair with as much aplomb as if he owned the place. Peggy Lullham had to repress one of the sarcasms she reserved for the uppity. After all, she was in his debt, and in view of the cost of the coat, was likely to remain so for some considerable time.

'Of course, I'm not really investigating you ladies, in any way,' began Royle, to get things straight. 'As I've said to Mrs Lullham here –' proprietary wave of the hand as if they had never met before – 'I realize you and the old gent were meeting for the first time, and that you two good ladies can't have much idea about motives, and that sort of thing. But it will be really interesting to hear what you made of the party, how you thought things went.' He paused for a moment, not used to speaking for such a length of time, but rather thinking he wasn't going to get much chance once these two got together. 'Of course, I have spoken to the academics, and to Miss Tambly, but they're not quite . . .'

'Ladies?' said Mrs Lullham with a nervous little laugh.

'Miss Tambly isn't what I call a woman at all,' said Mrs McKay. 'Did you notice her legs, Peggy? More like a footballer's than a woman's, I'd say. And those shoes!'

Royle slid further down into his chair, perfectly relaxed, and let it all slide over him.

'No wonder people are a bit chary about sending their girls to that dumpy school,' agreed Peggy. 'Not that it's as bad, somehow, as with boys. Still, I can't say I'd want a daughter of mine coming home looking like an armoured tank.'

'And behaving like one,' said Mrs McKay.

'Yes, it's not as though she had any social manners to set off her size, is it? She just barges in and says what she thinks without a by-your-leave, and heaven help you if you contradict her.'

'She does make me feel a bit as if she'd been one of the Belsen guards, or something.'

'Well, or course she was, in a way,' said Peggy Lullham, 'or at least a prison governor somewhere here, which is much the same thing. I believe that's why they gave her the job. But it's a bit thick of Lucy Wickham expecting one to meet her. I must say, I can never decide how I'm to talk to her, I mean, what sort of voice to use to her, and that sort of thing.'

'Of course the academics are like that in a way too. I'm never sure about them either.'

'Oh, I agree. The district has definitely gone downhill since they came, as we were saying the other night. You remember what a nice little *circle* we were in the old days, all like one big family as it were, even if we did have our disagreements now and then' (she had remembered inconveniently that she and Joan McKay had once gone eleven years without speaking to each other). 'But when I go to people's homes these days I keep seeing people I don't know. One can't be sure whether they're academics or real people, so I don't know whether to be friendly or just — kind.'

'I do so agree,' said Mrs McKay. 'I've seen so much of that Uni crowd, and been so disgusted that I've almost made up my mind not to send my Daphne there. You know, she's very literary — you can hardly get a word out of her when the *Woman's Weekly* arrives on Wednesdays. But then to think of her among all those weird types — well, no mother would welcome it, in my opinion. The trouble is, what else are we to do with her?

We thought of a finishing school, possibly Switzerland, you know. But then the Nolan girl came back from France married to the kitchen boy, and I've had to think again.'

'Of course they say he's a Count,' said Peggy Lullham, 'but you can still smell the onion on him.'

'You notice how the academics didn't mix the other night,' said Mrs McKay. 'They just collected together in a corner and talked about their own affairs − syllabuses or something as far as I could hear. They hardly exchanged a word with the rest of us.'

'But when they did, you wished they hadn't,' said Peggy Lullham. 'I told you about my Encounter, didn't I?'

'No. Do give.'

'Well, it was awfully stuffy in there, with all those cheap cigarettes and that bad wine, so I went out into the garden for a breather. You know I can never stand a fug after an hour or two.' (Mrs Lullham was famous for taking her secateurs to parties and thieving cuttings of other peoples rarities.) 'Well, I was just admiring Lucy Wickham's roses when what do you think I saw on the other side of the rose bed?'

'Don't know. What?'

'Just as near to me as you are this moment. That dirty, drunken man − what's his name? − Day, isn't it. One of Wickham's staff. And he was *urinating* on a rose bush.'

'He wasn't!'

'He was. Bold as brass. I shouted: "Don't do that; that's a Dusky Maiden." And he said: "First time I've ever heard it called that." I could have sunk through the ground. I didn't know where to look.'

'It's funny, isn't it? You wouldn't expect academics to be so *crude*, would you? But they are!'

'Oh, they are, most of them. Not the old boy, of course. Quite a different type of person altogether.'

'Yes, yes. More the old world type. You could imagine there might be breeding there somewhere.'

'Oh, you could see that.'

'He was bored stiff, like the rest of us.'

'Even Lucy wasn't making much headway with him after a time. He was hardly noticing her.'

'And usually she's so good like that. I'll give her that – she can make people feel at home, if she tries. I suppose it's a necessary virtue if you're so . . . undiscriminating in who you entertain. I'm sorry for her, though, in a way. That husband of hers isn't much help to her. A bit of a nonentity, I'd say.'

'Yes, just like old Turberville. It's not much encouragement to a woman, especially if she's obviously breaking her back to push herself forward.'

'As Lucy Wickham is.'

'Her trouble is she doesn't know what she wants. Half the time she wants to get in with the graziers, and with our lot in general; half the time you can see that at heart she despises us – because really all she wants is for that husband of hers to get a job in Sydney or Melbourne, not that I can see it happening.'

'Nor can I. After all, they must have *some* standards in Universities like that.'

Miraculously they paused for breath, and Peggy Lullham caught sight of Inspector Royle's empty glass. She grabbed at it and Royle started forward and grunted, giving every sign of waking up from a discontented doze.

'Much obliged to you, ma'am,' he said as she bustled out to the kitchen to refill his glass. 'Then I'll have to be going.'

'Was there anything else you wanted to know, Inspector?' asked Joan McKay, obviously under the impression that they had been answering questions from him for the past hour, and that he had been listening. Royle tried to give the impression that he had, but was not quite sure how to, since he had been far away for the last five minutes in dreams he would hardly like to describe in polite company.

'I'm not sure, ma'am,' he said, reaching greedily for his

141

new glass, and sinking greedily into it. 'Most of what I wanted to know, I've got by now, I think.' And he drew his blue-shirted arms gratefully across the ring of foam around his mouth, stopping guiltily half-way, suddenly realizing this was not supposed to be the thing.

'I imagine you've got your ideas of who it was, haven't you?' asked Peggy Lullham.

'Oh yes, ma'am,' said Royle with childish cunning. 'We definitely have got our ideas. Of course, one doesn't want to be premature, but I think I can say we've got our eye on someone, yes, ma'am.'

'I just hope it's one of the academics,' said Mrs McKay. 'I'd put my money on that new one − that spotty little creep just out from Oxford − what's his name?'

'Now that's most interesting, ma'am,' said Royle, without the slightest suspicion of a guilty conscience that he might be playing foul by his new ally. 'You'd plump for him, would you? Why would that be, now?'

'If you're still spotty at that age, there must be something wrong with you.'

'You're right there, Joan,' said Peggy Lullham sagely. 'Mentally wrong, physiologically wrong.'

Royle downed his beer and stood up. Women's intuition didn't seem likely to come up trumps this time.

'One last thing,' he said. 'When did you ladies get home? On the night of the party, that is?'

'Oh, that's easy,' said Peggy. 'I drove Joan. Her husband was to fetch her, but he was doing a business deal in town. We rang Beecher's from the Wickhams', but he was still busy, so we drove home together.'

'When would that make it you left, then?'

'Well, about ten minutes after the old boy, so far as I remember,' said Joan McKay.

'Arriving home . . .'

'About a quarter to twelve, give a quarter of an hour or so either way,' said Peggy. 'Can't say I looked at the clock. Anyway, I gave Joan the car, and she drove on.'

'Anybody vouch for you?'

Both ladies looked somewhat affronted.

'Vouch for us?' said Peggy. 'Well, the Wickhams saw us leave – they came to the road to wave.'

'That's not quite what I meant, ma'am. Was your husband awake when you arrived home?'

'He was *not*, Inspector. My husband gets up a seven to see to the property. He was fast asleep when I got back.'

'And you, ma'am?' pursued Royle, turning to Joan McKay.

'Well, there was no one there when I got home. All the servants were in bed, of course. No, I'm afraid I'll have to be unvouched for, as you call it, Inspector.'

'Oh well,' said Royle philosophically. 'I don't suppose it matters. It's just a matter of form. Thanks for the grog. I don't reckon I'll be needing to trouble you ladies again.'

He shook hands all round with a smarmy smile, hoping to re-establish himself in the ladies' favour after this ruthless bout of questioning, and lumbered off through the front door in the direction of his car. Peggy Lullham and Joan McKay went hesitantly towards the window and watched him go. He started off with a burst, adding a thick cloud of dust to the already dusty atmosphere. The two women watched until the car became a mere speck, seeming a little uncertain of themselves, as if they both wanted to say something to the other, but weren't quite sure how to approach the subject. Finally, as they turned back into the lounge, they caught each other's eyes, and Joan McKay said quickly in a burst:

'*Was* your husband in when you got home, Peg?'

'No. What about yours?'

'He didn't get in all night. And I can't get a thing out of him – can you?'

CHAPTER FOURTEEN

Dark Interlude

The relief with which Royle realized that he had now interviewed all the people at the party for Belville-Smith was tempered by the thought that he had 'got' nothing out of any of them. The non-violent method of interrogation had its drawbacks, as he had always suspected but had never hitherto had a chance to test. One might say that there had emerged from the interviews hints, impressions, suggestions – one might, but as far as Royle was concerned it would not be true, because none of these things had fastened themselves on to his own consciousness. That delicate amalgam of feelings and intuitions which in most detective stories seems to take the place of solid evidence, or at any rate to precede it, was not a chemical process likely to take place in the mind of Royle. Some of those interviewed he had liked (in the sense that he knew how to deal with them); others he had disliked (in the sense that he did not know how to deal with them, and that they were the objects of his prejudice). He was quite willing to believe that those whom he liked were improbable murderers – at least of elderly Professors from England – and that those whom he disliked were probably the killers, or that one of them was. But beyond that lay a great blankness, and he knew that before the case could even get to court he was going to have to get a lot more to go on than that. In fact, he was going to have to back up his prejudices with some hard evidence, and of that he had not a scrap.

It was consciousness of this that soured his temper on the drive home from the Lullhams' rather down-at-heel property. As more and more estates assumed a neglected and unpromising aspect, due to the drought, Royle sensed a drying-up of potential income. He belched beery smells into the hot, stuffy car, and thought dark thoughts. He threaded his way, still at fifty miles an hour, among the right-angled back roads until he got to the police station, and pulled up outside with a screech − because like a child he still thought that was the only impressive way to stop a car. He slammed the door when he got out, but walked slowly and morosely up to the front door of the building, a low, rambling old house whose new officialdom sat lightly on it. It had once belonged to one of the city's mayors who had, in the nineteen-twenties, bankrupted himself (and nearly done the same for the city) in the building of it. As he pushed his way into the large waiting-room which was immediately inside the front door, a room full of imposing posters about regulations which nobody obeyed and wanted men whom nobody expected to catch, he heard the usual sounds of cards being shuffled in the little off-duty room nearby. He also heard the scarcely less usual sound of somebody being beaten up somewhere down at the other end of the building.

'Tell 'em to keep it a bit quiet, can you, Jim,' he snapped to the sergeant on duty who was shuffling papers at the desk. 'They don't need to stop − just shove a gag in or something.'

'Right-ee-ho,' said the sergeant. 'Feeling under the weather? I've never known you to have a hangover.'

' 'Snot that. It's this bloody murder. I've got to sit down and have a real good think.'

The sergeant was immensely impressed.

'Gee, that's tough. Well, best of luck.' And he went off in the direction of the screams and thumps.

Royle gave a grunt of self-pity, and was just proceeding in the direction of his office when he felt his shirt-sleeves being tugged from behind. Sensing an affront to his cloth, he turned and was annoyed to see a thin, old, tiny aboriginal woman. He had noticed and not noticed her as he came in, in the way that one does notice and not notice old aboriginal women. She had been sitting over by the door, but now she had come up to him. She was looking straight into his red, blotchy face, and seemed fairly used to the sort of stench that he emitted from his mouth. It momentarily flashed through his mind that there could be no reason for the way his wife flinched at the smell of his beery breath.

'That's my son,' said the old woman, pointing towards the room at the back of the house.

'Is it, now?' said Royle unsympathetically. 'Well, he'll know better in future, won't he?'

'He ain't done nothing,' said the woman.

'If he's innocent he has nothing to fear,' said Royle. It was a phrase he had read somewhere and thought might be useful. A scream from the back of the room immediately proved him wrong. Apparently Royle's mates were having a last fling before giving him his peace for meditation, for immediately afterwards silence descended.

'You make them stop doin' him over and I tell you sumpen,' said the old woman urgently.

'What could you tell me, for Chrissake?' said Royle, looking at her with contempt and trying to shrug her off. His present investigation gave him an immense disgust for the world of petty Abo crimes which had previously occupied his time and skills. But she kept her fingers on the sleeve of his shirt.

'That ther murder,' she said. 'I can tell you sumpen about that.'

'What murder?' said Royle. 'Has there been another knifing down at the reserve? Anyway, if there has, I don't want to know about it. Tell the sergeant here, when he comes back. I've got my hands full at the moment, thank you very much.'

'That murder at the Yarumba,' said the woman insistently. 'Old white man.'

Royle stopped in his tracks, but his congenital disbelief of the non-white soon reasserted itself.

'Bloody likely you'd know anything about that,' he said. 'That's no Abo case. You're just shamming to get your son out of a beating-up.' He paused. 'Not that anyone's beating him up,' he added virtuously. 'I expect he attacked them in there, and they're having trouble in restraining him.'

Aboriginals were very prone, single-handed, to attack six or seven enormous Australian policemen, and so furious was the struggle that they often got considerably damaged in the process of being restrained. Everyone had considerable sympathy for the police in their difficult job.

'Them big fellers in it,' said the woman cunningly. 'Missa Turberville, Missa Lullham, Missa McKay. All them big boys. They say you go and see all them people.'

Royle didn't think it necessary to correct her as to whom he had gone to see.

'Well, so what?' he said.

'They all in sumpen together,' said the woman. 'Ah don't know zacly what it is, but it's sumpen 'portant. Them big fellers they got hold of Johnny Marullah up at the camp.'

'That sort of person,' said Royle with dignity, 'wouldn't touch Johnny Marullah with a bloody barge pole. Come off it.'

147

'You go see. Tomorrow night. They all go out to the Turbervilles'. Two o'clock in the night, all them big fellers. They doin' sumpen there. You go see.'

'What – Turberville, McKay and Lullham?'

'Yeah, them and some others: Nolan, Coogan, some more.'

'Take something to get all that lot friendly with each other,' said Royle thoughtfully. 'Where is this thing, whatever it is, taking place? At the house? It's a big property that.'

'Don't know, sah.'

'Strikes me you don't know much about it at all,' said Royle. 'If you're wasting my time . . .'

'You tell them stop hit my boy,' said the woman, coming unpleasantly close.

'OK,' said Royle, pushing her away and going towards his office. 'OK, but don't you stay around this town if you've made a fool of me, because that boy of yours life won't be worth five cents.'

He slammed the door to his room, and got on the phone to his colleagues in the back room.

'Here, lay off that Abo, can you, Fred? I don't know what he's done, but can you just let him go?'

He screwed up his face at the surprised response from the other end. No one likes being unjustly accused of softness.

'Yeah, I know I'm not an Abo-lover as a rule, but I've got my reasons . . . OK, OK, just another five minutes. Don't want to spoil your fun. But somewhere it doesn't show, can't you? And then let him go. Right?'

He banged down the phone, and sat back in his chair, puzzling his brain into a beery, speculative, questioning doze.

CHAPTER FIFTEEN

After Midnight

Over the grey-green Australian landscape there hung an immense darkness. It was now nearly one o'clock, and an almost complete silence reigned. Up to an hour or so ago there had been sounds from occasional cars driven along and around the main road by drinkers returning from Drummondale to their insufficiently grateful wives and children, and from these cars had come the sounds of badly-changed gears, snatches of alcoholic song and occasional curses before they faded into the stillness. Now, even these typical rural noises were stilled, which made the tentative bleats which now and then escaped the dreaming sheep in the vicinity doubly eerie. At one point the hoot of an owl very clost to his shoulder had nearly made Royle jump out of his skin.

He was in any case in a quite unnatural condition of wakefulness. For a start he had had nothing to drink. Then he had not only slept at home the night before, but had remained much of the morning as well, having rung up Mrs Beecham (whose turn it was) the day before to say that the romantic highlight of her week would not be taking place. His family was greatly surprised and not at all pleased by this change in his habits. He had sworn at his wife when she asked for the fourth time whether she should call the doctor. Once he had got himself up, he spent most of the rest of the day glowing with virtue, though by eight o'clock virtue was fighting a losing battle with thirst. When the proprietor of Mackinnon's, the rival establishment to Beecher's, had hailed him as he walked along the main street and invited him in for a schooner it had required an effort almost supernatural to refuse, but refuse he had. To compensate he had explained that duty was, for this one night, imperative, but that he would be taking up the offer in the very near future. The proprietor had retreated, puzzled, into the saloon bar, where Royle was a regular. It was the general opinion there that something very big must be on that night.

By rights, then, Royle ought to have been in tip-top form; but the way his hands shook, and the desperation with which he was dragging on his Pall Mall filter, both suggested that he was far from happy in his mind.

For a start, though he thought of himself as a man of the great outdoors – as all Australians do – he did not, in fact, like it much, especially after dark, and especially once you got off the main road. He had planned the operation very carefully, and had decided that the best place for his car was in the little spinney half a mile from the main road on the track to Kenilworth, the Turberville property. It had seemed ideal in prospect, but now, hidden by trees some yards from the dirt track, and with a funny feeling that beasts of various sorts were looking at him (and perhaps laughing at him as well), he wished he were a good deal closer to civilization, with a few of his mates within cooee in case of an emergency. They weren't much use, but they were better than this damned solitude. And then, though he had tried to work up a fug in the car by smoking incessantly, he was distinctly cold. At least, he kept shivering, and that must mean that he was cold.

In point of fact he was in the sort of situation in which a man wonders whether he is being a bloody fool.

Certainly he felt he had taken every precaution to see whether he was doing the right thing or not. The trouble was, he couldn't bring in the Abo and thump the truth out of him, since what he wanted was a dramatic, red-handed catch – of whoever it was, doing whatever it was. He knew Johnny Marullah vaguely – a smart little near full-blood who did occasional jobs on the Turberville property. He was considered something of a character, and was much in demand from the idiots out at the Uni who were supposed to be investigating aboriginal languages, which Royle thought the biggest bloody waste of bloody tax-payers' money he had ever known in all his bloody life, as he had frequently said to an admiring audience in various places of alcoholic refreshment throughout the town. But he had not often been through the hands of the police, and therefore he knew little about him beyond this. It taxed his small imagining powers well beyond their limits to think what Turberville and the rest could want with him, and what whatever it was could have to do with the murder. He just had to hope and pray that the old crone hadn't been seizing at a straw. By now she and her goddamned son would have gone walkabout well out of reach of his revengeful fist if she had been having him on.

Failing a talk to Marullah, he had done the best he could. He had talked to all the other policemen he could lay his hands on (except those superior to him in rank, to whom he was afraid of exposing himself in some sort of silliness) to see if he could get any kind of line as to what was going on among the grazing fraternity. He got little more than that most of them had been seen drunk and disorderly at various times over the past month, and that some of them had gone on a lavish spending-spree when their drought-relief cheques had arrived. There was nothing out of the ordinary there. Not worth the trouble of asking.

However, Sergeant Brady had been able to provide

something a mite more tangible. Like most policemen, he found out what was going on in the town not through his own efforts – he was occupied for much of the day in poker at the station – but through those of his wife, a sharp little woman with too much time on her hands. She was not only a one-woman bush telegraph, but she was generally held to have rendered bugging devices an unnecessary luxury for the Drummondale force. She had been standing at the drinks counter in the Darcy supermarket the day before, immediately behind Mrs McKay and Mrs Dutton, another grazier's wife. She had been able to pick up very little of their conversation, because she was well known even outside her own circle as the longest pair of ears in town, and the two women, who were well outside her class, shut up as soon as they spotted her. But she gathered, putting two and two together, that they were talking about their husbands going out at night. Not going out in the evening, which would be too normal for remark, but at night. And she had been struck by the unusual earnestness of the two women.

'*Several* times in the last month,' Mrs McKay had said. The other woman had whispered, in a rather bewildered way, that all she had been able to get out of her husband was that he had been 'rehearsing', but she thought she must have misheard, because he certainly wasn't one for the amateur dramatics, and it seemed much more likely that what he had said had something to do with 'horses'.

'I heard mine make an appointment for Friday,' said Mrs McKay. 'But God knows he's never at home, so it could be something else altogether. All I know is, there's something up, but I can't for the life of me think what it could be.'

They had then caught sight of Mrs Brady's ears, and an iron curtain had descended. It had not been much to go on, but it was something. That evening Royle had got in touch with some of the Turberville station hands – by drinking at their expense in the Beecher's public bar – and had tried to milk them of anything they might know. He found them willing enough to talk without feeling any compunctions of feudal loyalty. They said that they had heard Turberville driving from the big house in the middle of the night, but that the general conjecture had been that he was going to sleep with his daughter-in-law, a luscious young Queenslander who generously made herself available to anyone who showed an interest. There seemed to be little evidence for this assumption except that she was there, she was willing, and what else would a man be doing in the middle of the night? But this didn't account for the rest of the grazing fraternity being involved? Royle was willing to believe that particular young woman would take them all on, but surely not all at once?

Some of the men from the Lullham property who had been in the bar were also questioned in Royle's hamfistedly casual way, and they had also thought that their lord and master might have been driving around in the middle of the night. But when Royle had got interested they had got increasingly cussed, for Royle had not been willing to buy them drinks in return for whatever information they could provide. They didn't know whether he'd been driving home or driving away from home, they didn't remember exactly what time it was they'd heard him, and anyway it was his bloody business and what's it bloody matter to you? Royle had damped down his inclination to thump them since he was conserving his strength, and had left the bar. That had been the night before, and that was all he had to go on. Sitting there shivering in his large dark police car, surrounded by bats and caustic-sounding birds, it did not seem much.

At least he wasn't the only one suffering, he thought.

Dotted around the surrounding emptiness were other cars, more or less well-hidden — or so he hoped. You never knew with the subordinates he had got: they could have put themselves in the wrong spot, they could have downed too many beers and dozed off, they could have got side-tracked by a variety of amorous adventures offered by Drummondale. They could even simply have forgotten. Luckily he could be fairly sure of Sergeant Malone, who lived near the road to the Lullham and McKay properties. He had merely been detailed to skulk in his front garden all night. On the road to six or seven other fair-sized properties in the vicinity, or just off them, he had posted men with walkie-talkies, either in police-cars or on foot, depending on whether there was suitable cover or not. He had already heard from several of them, but he was keeping communication down to a minimum. Heaven help them if they got caught. The last thing he wanted to jeopardize was the relationship between the police and the grazing community. It was, to his mind, the rock on which Australian civilization was built. Not even his own promotion would be worth any disruption of the bond, since the likely increase in his salary would certainly not equal the amount every year screwed out of the rural gentry for one reason or another.

All in all it was a tricky, uncomfortable business. One thing Royle did not like was taking risks: he had a devout belief in the idea that one didn't hit someone bigger than oneself, nor try bullying someone more powerful. These precepts had for him a force almost biblical, and it was due to this canny philosophy that Royle's career, in spite of a few regrettable set-backs, had on the whole been one of onwards and upward, in spite of his evident and invincible stupidity. But in the present case, he could see that he was in the middle of a situation in which he could very well land himself (as he put it in his own mind) in the shits. And what made it worse was that he could not, at the moment, see any possibility at all of blaming anyone else for it.

A little red light on his dashboard showed one of his men trying to get through. He stubbed out his cigarette in an already overful ashtray and picked up his receiver.

'Royle here.'

'Brady, sir. There's a car just left the Nolan property – Murrawidgee. Went very quiet and slow for the first few minutes, then speeded up when he was away from the house.'

Royle breathed a sigh of relief. He had been tormented by the thought that he, as well as several of his men, would be sitting like dummies around the landscape all night without so much as a cheep from any of the people they were watching. He was no wiser about *what* was going to happen, but at least he was now pretty sure that something was.

'Fine,' he said. 'Everything else quiet over there? No one awake in the house?'

'No lights, anyway. I'm too far away to hear anything, but there's definitely no signs. What do I do now?'

'You can come away. You might as well get here as soon as you can – you could be useful.'

'Look, cobber,' said Brady in a practised whine, 'I'm stuck up a bloody tree with bloody magpies dive-bombing me every few seconds, and me car is three miles away where you told me to put it. It'll be bloody hours before I can get over to you.'

'Oh, you can bugger off home,' said Royle impatiently. 'No bloody initiative, that's your trouble. The others will be coming, so we can do without you and good riddance.'

No sooner had he cut off Brady, and put through a mental prayer to the Eternal Superintendent that the magpies be allowed to get his balls, than the rest of his men started coming through. At least they gave Royle the satisfaction of knowing that he really was on to something – some sort of conspiracy, for whatever purpose. They all had a similar tale to tell. The men they were watching had driven off, usually in a decidedly surreptitious manner; some had coasted until they were away from the house, some had kept their lights off as long as that was feasible, some had gone to the lengths of walking to a car parked well away from the house. None of his subordinates seemed at all anxious to join him, though Constable Rudge, the most junior, assured him that he'd be there as soon as he possibly could – granted that he was twenty-five miles away, two miles from his car, and he *had* heard a nasty knocking in the engine on the way out from town. It was by now getting through to Royle that a certain reluctance was being manifested.

The last to contact him was Sergeant Malone, apparently ensconced in the middle of a rhododendron bush, or else rubbing a leafy branch across the mouth of his microphone to give his story dramatic verisimilitude. The McKay and Lullham cars, he said, had come out of their turning in procession, and had sped off in the direction of Kenilworth. McKay had obviously liased with Lullham on the way, and the two cars had kept rather nervously close to one another as long as they were on the gravel track leading to the main road.

'So they'll be with you in about twenty minutes I'd guess,' concluded Sergeant Malone.

'And so will you,' said Royle sharply. 'Get in the car, and keep well behind them. Above all, don't for God's sake let them know they're being followed.'

'Aw, chief, give over,' whined Malone. 'You know the wife doesn't like me being out late at night. And the rheumatics are playing me up something cruel tonight . . .'

'Get here fast,' said Royle.

'I've got a doctor's certif. . .'

Royle cut him off with an expletive which sounded into the darkness. He knew what was up now. They'd all talked it over, and they'd decided he was making a fool of himself. THEY'D decided – the incompetent nincompoops. They couldn't even recognize a parking offence unless you rubbed their noses in it. And then they'd also decided they wanted no more part in the business that was absolutely necessary. He knew why. They were no keener than himself to get on the wrong side of the local nobility. True they were not in a position to make such a good thing of it as he was. Mere chickenfeed, really. Still, they could hope for the odd free beer, the condescending greeting in the street which so gratified the wife and sent her stock up with the neighbours. And every one of them knew that if promotion came – and on the whole no consideration of stupidity, corruption or physical incapacity could ever stop it coming – this would mean one more toe for them on the jolly old gravy train. The inferiority of their rank did not stop them having great expectations. So they'd decided to do their little bit and then skulk off home, leaving him well and truly in the rural lurch. That was loyalty for you! That was the spirit of the service! That was mateship!

Royle sat in the dark of his police car boiling with the virtuous indignation of one who has been played a well-deserved dirty trick. The more he thought about it, the less he thought the Australian police force deserved him. He was a damned fine officer, doing a damned fine job of work, and cursed with the idlest bunch of inferiors you could meet in a month of Sundays. But before five minutes had passed he was interrupted in his halo-construction work when he perceived a pencil-thin light from a distant car. It was proceeding off the main road, and coming along the broad gravel track towards Kenilworth. A minute later there was another, taking

the same route. Royle got out of his car, only remembering at the last moment not to bang the door shut. The
twigs cracked under him, as well they might, but he
darted into position under a large gum-tree, and stood
with his body against the trunk, waiting and watching.
He began in his mind to tot off the cars as they crept by.

The first to crawl past him along the track was
Coogan from Fairlands, and then came Nolan from
Murrawidgee, both of them driving cautiously and
using only parking lights. At any other time he might
have thought that they must be drunk to the point of
incapability, this being the only state in which
Australians willingly drive so slowly and hesitantly. But
clearly this was different: here they were obviously out
to hide their presence from the observation of someone
at the main Turberville property, and perhaps from the
residents of the houses of the younger married Turbervilles – or at any rate from the womenfolk at these
places. Both cars, so far as he could see through the
Stygian gloom of the night, contained only the driver.
This was not business for women, then. But if this
business wasn't drinking, what was it?

After a few minutes the Lullham car turned on to the
Kenilworth track, closely followed by McKay's new
Holden, a puce, green and purple monstrosity much
admired in Drummondale. Lullham's driving was
hesitant in the extreme, and Royle heard curses from
McKay's vehicle, so presumably he was incommoded by
the erratic stops and starts of the car in front. As that
little procession faded into the distance two more cars
came into evidence from the main road. Both of these
were comparatively well-driven – one belonged to
Gordon from Glen Angus, the other to Dutton from
Burraloo. Both were reasonably young men, and
Gordon was not long out from Scotland, a thin, craggy,
sarcastic man with a nasty tongue for what he regarded
as incompetence or idleness (that is, for those qualities

which Royle regarded proper evaluation of difficulties and sensible conservation of energies). Royle had once copped the rough side of that tongue, and for the first time in his career came close to hitting a grazier. It was Royle's opinion that Gordon had never in his life touched anything stronger than whisky marmalade, and if he was invited it didn't seem likely that drinking was the order of the day. Dutton too, though he could knock it back on occasions, was not one of the beeriest of his breed, and was hardly likely to give up a night's rest for a mere booze-up when he could have as much as he might need more comfortably at home.

Lastly, driving not wisely or too well, came Pryce-Jones of Llanuwchllyn, a man so ordinary that nobody could find anything whatsoever to say about him except that he got very sentimental when drunk, and that his property was unpronounceable. That was the lot. Now the difficult bit began.

As the Pryce-Jones car, a fawn Cortina, disappeared along the dark dusty road towards Kenilworth, Royle emerged from his natural cover and skulked towards his station wagon. Opening up the back, he dragged from it an ancient police bicycle, which he then put on his shoulders and humped to the road. Earlier in the day he had checked and double-checked this antiquated machine, and had only been dissuaded from having a trial spin round the back garden by the thought that one of his daughters might see. Took you back, that bicycle did, he thought. This one hadn't been used for at least twenty years so far as he could see. Police bicycles had made him the man he was today − more or less − them and Grafton's lager. Now he stealthily took it through the trees, set it four-square on the road, and heaved his bulk over the bar. This was the way to travel, was the thought that flashed through his mind; this brought back the old days in Newcastle when the blue uniform was still new on him and when he was first realizing that women who didn't find *him* attractive did find *him in it* moderately acceptable. This bicycle was part of his past, he thought, with an unaccustomed access of sentimentality.

His first conscious thought as he settled himself into the saddle was that, though he was well-padded in the posterior, this did not prevent the seat from feeling exceptionally hard. It just wasn't like driving the Holden. They built them tough in the seat in those days, he thought. Then, as he put his feet to the pedals and set off in stealthy pursuit of the cars he was suddenly struck with the notion that bicycling *was* the sort of skill you could forget. So far he had been imagining it was just like swimming, and that once thrown in the deep end all his old proficiency would return. And yet this seemed like an entirely new sensation. It couldn't just be that a gravel lane on a dark night without lights was not the best situation in which to take up the art again. There was also the question of his weight: it seemed to have been redistributed since he last rode. Or, to put it bluntly, it had increased. And as a consequence it certainly didn't seem as easy as it was to – oops – keep – oops – steady. He put his feet to the ground momentarily to right himself. If he couldn't improve on that performance it might have been quieter to stick with the car. He felt he would soon have to turn on his cycle-lamp. He had thought he'd be able to rely on moonlight alone, but the moon was far from full, and it didn't seem to be putting much effort into its shine. The path stretched ahead like a vague, shimmering river, shifting and changing. If he wasn't careful he'd be into the – ouch, damn, blast, Christ Almighty – into the ditch.

He got up stiffly, and switched on the little lamp at the front of his machine. Hesitantly and painfully he clambered back on. He wondered whether walking might not be better than this, but he hadn't walked more than ten yards at a time for so many years that he was

160

reluctant to put his feet to the test. Slowly, waveringly, like an elderly drunk, he proceeded along the bumpy track. Every jerk told in every muscle of his body, and he infinitely regretted the friendly upholstery of his police Holden which contrived to muffle the worst effects of Australian roads. Certainly he was becoming aware of muscles he had forgotten existed, muscles which he had not used since he was kicking around in his carry-cot, muscles which had slept undisturbed as the Kraken virtually the whole length of his life. Tomorrow was going to be hell. Tomorrow he was going to sleep stretched rigid on his bed, and woe betide anyone who demanded activity of him – let alone common civility. It was nearly a month since he had had his last sickie; this one would be a genuine one, so he'd spin it out.

He pushed his way forward, slowly, heavily. It was like being on a treadmill. Now he realized how ghastly that must be he was all the more in favour of bringing it back. At last his flapping trousers – he had, of course, forgotten that there were such things as trouser-clips – caught in the spokes, and after a tense moment of apparent suspension in mid-air, brought him down head first into a bank of loose gravel at the side of the road. For a moment he lay there, thinking his last moments were come, and wishing they would pass quickly and bring him into that policeman's Elysium he so richly deserved. Getting up, holding his side, and spitting genteelly and tentatively so as not to break the silence, he kicked his cycle to the side of the road, where some days later it was found by one of the Turberville grandchildren, who examined it as if it were a relic of a long-forgotten civilization but, failing to see to what use it could be put, left it to rust where it was.

From now on, Royle would have to rely on his feet. He found that they did still put themselves on in front of the other in a fairly automatic way, leaving him time to think of the selfless way he was sacrificing his own comfort in the cause of justice. In little more than ten minutes he was in sight of Kenilworth, but even as he became conscious of its looming bulk, he realized that it was not there he should be making for. He strained his eyes to look for parked cars, but he could not make out any. That was what he had expected: if this was a matter which the various wives were to be kept out of, as seemed to be the case, the men would hardly meet in a place where they would certainly be heard by that redoubtable old trout Mrs Turberville. The question flitted across his mind: why were they being excluded, these formidable wives? Usually they were in on everything. Was it because they were too narrow-minded; because they were too sober; because they were too sensible? Even as he started to ponder this one he heard to his right, away in the distance, a light sound.

It was a sound he was puzzled to identify — was it animal or human? Was it a car or some sort of musical instrument? Just ahead of him was a track, branching off to the right from the main gravel road which would lead him straight to Kenilworth. Bending down he peered at the surface, and noticed it had been recently disturbed: cars had passed along there recently, he felt sure, and had turned off. Where to? This side track didn't lead to anybody's property, that was for sure. As far as he knew it ended up in a rather pretty little natural valley, with a few gum-trees and some smooth rocks for sitting on. Nothing spectacular as scenery, but pleasantly regular, and standing out from the prevailing Australian sameness. He believed it had been used for picnics by the local Country Party supporters association, and once the local wives had tried to get up a country danc-ing club which had met there once or twice but which had collapsed amid a considerable amount of male ridicule. At any rate this lot wouldn't be doing Scottish reels, unless Mr Gordon had an even more effective tongue than he had realized. But what sort of business could they have there at this time of night? He sighed, and pressed on.

Another ten minutes' solid walk and Royle was feeling still more fed up and distinctly unsure of himself. He was not usually a jumpy person, as everyone knew. Though a physical coward, he had too little imagination to think every shadow was a murderer or a poltergeist. He was afraid of real threats, but not of shadows. But this was something that he had never experienced before. From time to time, proceeding it seemed from the darkness ahead, there had come to his ears – sounds that meant nothing to him, sounds which connected themselves with nothing that he knew, but which wrapped themselves round him in the night. They were isolated sounds, sometimes followed by similar ones which sounded like imitations. They said no more to him than would the music of Anton Webern, but they left him similarly irritated and uneasy. Finally, just as his steps were becoming hesitant, and he was in a classic state of indecision as to whether to continue forward or go back – and with all the indications being that he would flee – he became conscious of the dim outline of a car. Going forwards towards it, he struck his shin on a fender, and cursed outright – the words luckily being drowned by another of those isolated notes, this time nearer and louder. He looked around, and realized there were vehicles all around him – large, capacious graziers' cars, most of them parked around a large gum-tree. Suddenly he knew that he could not bear the torment of not knowing exactly what was going on. His mind was made up for him, and his course would have to be forward.

Stealthily he made his way through the little knot of cars. He realized that this was the end of the track – the road circled round the tree, and then proceeded back the way it came. On Royle's left the land rose gently, to dip down more steeply on the other side to form the natural valley. It was here, clearly, that the men were congregated. It was from here that the occasional note still emerged – menacing, but somehow preparatory, like a clearing of the throat. Reluctantly Royle turned to his left. There was a path up to the summit he felt sure, but it might be as well to keep off it, just in case the men were looking in that direction, expecting someone else. He would have to go round a bit before putting his head over the top. The going was a bit rough at the spot where he chose to ascend. He carefully measured each step in advance, and thought out where to place his foot. He didn't want a twig to crack if he could help it: if those men were in anything like his state, they would be quite unusually aware of sounds in their vicinity. He did not even swear when he trod in something soft that felt very like cow dung. He had not known he was capable of such self-control.

As he pressed on and neared the summit, the occasional, isolated notes ceased, but in their place he heard something else: movements, scuffles, a muttered curse or two. Confident that these noises would cover his own, Royle increased his speed, and had nearly gained the ridge of the slope when he was transfixed by a sound which made his hair bristle on his scalp, and sent goose-pimples down the fatty length of his body, as if he had suddenly had the cold shower turned on him. It was a noise like nothing he had ever heard – menacing still, but at the same time soulful, rhythmical, as if imploring something. It wasn't drunken singing, it wasn't rugby-club celebrations. It was . . .

Suddenly it came to him. For once in his life Royle solved a mystery without having the solution thrust in front of his nose – albeit the mystery was a tiny one, and its solution was never to contribute to the official recognition that he craved. He was no longer inhibited by fear. Speeding up still further he approached the summit and dropped swiftly to his stomach. The sight that met his delighted, incredulous eyes was one to gratify the minds of those who loved to watch the mingling and fruitful interaction of civilizations old and new.

In the middle of the valley, shouting enthusiastically to the four winds, was a dark naked body. In one hand was some sort of musical instrument, in the other something long and deadly — a primitive weapon which he was waving. The figure was capering round, as if in ecstasy. Around him was a ring of figures whose abandonment was apparently less complete. They were also waving what looked like broomstick handles, and were shifting from one foot to another with considerable embarrassment, like parents at a teenage party. They were shouting more or less in time to gesticulations from their leader. All of them were stripped to their underpants, and their movements became the more frenzied as the chill night air struck their bare skins and ate into their paunchy bodies. They chanted wildly, and as Royle lay watching, scarcely able to believe his eyes, they became more confident, more abandoned. Their song had all the heartfelt pathos of men who see their bank-balances daily diminishing.

Down in the valley Mr Guy Turberville, Mr Ben Lullham, Mr Tim McKay, Mr Pete Nolan, Mr Bert Coogan, Mr Alistair Gordon, Mr Geoff Dutton, Mr Gabby Johnson and Mr Andy Pryce-Jones, under the knowledgeable leadership of Mr Johnny Marullah, were beginning to perform the age-old Australian ceremony of rain-making.

CHAPTER SIXTEEN

Private Lives

Alice O'Brien was walking heavily up and down her study-cum-sitting-room in Daisy Bates College, peering short-sightedly at her bookshelf, her desk, in fact everywhere but at the sofa, where a thin, sandy-haired student of non-descript appearance was wringing her hands, a gesture which her literary studies had taught her was an appropriate sign of repentance. Alice was trying to work up her stern-housemistress face before going any further with the interview. By dint of sucking in her lips and throwing back her shoulders (a gesture she had seen Miss Tambly accomplish to perfection) she finally succeeded, and turned around in her tracks.

'What a *bloody* silly thing to do,' she said – it was a convention throughout the various colleges of the university that all acts of a criminal, spiteful, immoral or vicious nature were to be referred to as 'silly'. The theory seemed to be that if one made the erring students feel childish they would be rendered more amenable to discipline, though in fact it seemed more often to result in an unfortunate marriage of the appetites of an adult with the random destructiveness of a child.

166

'I *do* agree, Miss O'Brien,' said the Dickensian waif on the sofa. 'I do *so* agree.'

'Robbing the shops in town is one thing,' said Alice; 'they fleece the students right and left all through the year, so you could say they ask for it in a way . . .'

'They *do*,' said the girl, with an air of committing this remarkable piece of moral tutoring to memory.

'. . . but pinching things from a fellow student is another thing altogether . . .'

'I quite see that,' said the student, having another quick wring.

'. . . especially as you were bound to be caught out as soon as you wore the things.'

'I didn't intend to wear them till I got home for the vac,' said the student sharply, apparently stung by the aspersion on her intelligence. 'But Norm O'Farrell had invited me to the Menzies Ball, and when my long skirt and blouse didn't come back from the dry cleaners, I hadn't any choice.'

'That doesn't alter the moral aspect at all,' said Alice.

'No, I *do* see that,' said the girl, reverting to her chosen role, and looking more like the Marchioness every minute. 'If you asked me why I did it, in the first place, I just couldn't tell you.'

This was exactly what Alice had been going to ask her, and she had quickly to think up another question.

'*How* did you do it?' she asked rather wildly.

'Eh?' said the Marchioness, caught off her pious guard.

'Er, how did you get in to Kathy Fowler's room? I gather it was locked at the time.'

'Oh, I used a hairpin. You must know how easy it is . . .'

'No, I didn't actually. What do you do?'

The Marchioness plunged a much-wrung hand into her hair, and started a demonstration.

'Show me on my door,' said Alice, peering rather

confusedly. 'If it is as easy as all that, I ought to know how these things are done.'

'Glad to oblige,' said the Marchioness.

Bill Bascomb came in from Hall, flung his gown on his bed, and went straight to the full sherry-flagon with which he had equipped himself earlier in the day. This was going to be an arduous evening. Waiting for him after his afternoon trudge through the drearier stretches of restoration 'comedy' had been a thick envelope of manuscripts and photocopies from his friend Jim Timmins of the *Oxford Mail*. He would have missed dinner on a normal day, but the fact that a visiting Professor of English from Melbourne was dining there changed his mind: he cherished the hope that other parts of Australia were less of a living death than the part he had happened to land in, and he had adopted the policy of building bridges wherever possible. However, any thoughts of bridges thrown out in the Melbourne direction had been abandoned after some incautious remarks he had made about Dr Leavis had led to a frosting-over which no amount of social chit-chat had been able to remove. So now he intended to console himself for a misspent hour and a half with sherry and gossip.

Jim Timmins was a journalist who believed in saturation coverage. He was usually sent by his editors to investigate problems of incredible complexity, which kept him away from the office for weeks. The results usually appeared when news was short, either because it was the silly season, or at other dry times such as the last days of December. His investigations of the state of college kitchens had once made the whole town throw up its Christmas fare. He was the only journalist on the paper who could make two columns out of a minor motor accident. Certainly his literary merits hardly included the pithy saying or the apt summing up. He had filled up page after page with what he had

168

discovered, such as it was, and his commentary was as voluminous as a *Hamlet* editor's, though hardly as imaginative. Bill Bascomb spread it all out over his coffee-table, took a couple of quick gulps of sherry, and settled in to it. As he read on, he was surprised to find that he was not surprised. Somehow, all this was very much what he had expected from these people. There was a dull shock of recognition, but little leaping of the heart at the manifold variety of human folly.

Professor Wickham, as befitted his status, had by far the largest folder. His university career had begun in 1948, when Oxford was still full of ex-servicemen. For his first year he had been unmarried, though he was already engaged to Lucy, whom he had obstinately insisted on calling his 'forces' sweetheart', to everyone's embarrassment. He had lived in college – the college being Oriel. He had come there with a first-class degree from Australia, but in spite of this he had made very little impression. 'Of course, the competition was hot in those days,' said one of his contemporaries, now a city-councillor and Liberal candidate somewhere in East Anglia, 'but even in an average year, you got the impression he'd have to work hard to be mediocre.' Apparently he had only scraped through Prelims, but that was not uncommon for bright students, and at the end of his first year he had married. Lucy Wickham had been escorted from Australia by some Caroline-Chisholm in-reverse, an arrangement master-minded by Professor Wickham's family who suspected her morals, but after the wedding ceremony she seemed to have reverted to the happy amorality of the milieu from which she came.

'Here I'm having to rely on gossip that can't be checked,' said Jim Timmins, with unjournalistic caution. Uncheckable gossip had it that after the Wickhams had set up house in a flat in Cowley Road the family budget had been eked out by Lucy, who had made herself discreetly available to a few selected 'friends' while her husband fought for a place in the cold and crowded libraries and lecture-rooms. This activity was pleasantly arranged on a quite un-professional level, and no one was quite certain how far her husband was aware of it. Uncheckable gossip also had it that Wickham's old scout at Oriel had helped in making this service known to various gilded youths whose family fortunes had survived the war and the aftermath of socialist austerity (austerity which Lucy was apparently in the habit of comparing rather bitterly to conditions back home, which had not endeared her to those healthy young men living on near-starvation rations who were her husband's contemporaries). Jim had visited the aforementioned scout, now retired, but beyond the fact that he had a disreputable eye, and was living in a poverty less extreme than that usually ordained by the Oxford colleges for their faithful servants, he had been able to get out of him almost nothing of substance.

'Confidentiality is everything in our job, just like with doctors, and lawyers, and gossip-writers,' the worthy old retainer with the disreputable eye had explained, downing the last drops of a pint of thick and expensive beer; 'and if you once let that go by the board, where are you? I mean, where are you? Yes, I will have another pint, thank you very much. Same again, Charley. No, what I will say of Mr Wickham is this: he was a very nice gentleman. A very nice gentleman indeed. And that's what I'd say of all the other gentlemen I've served. Very nice gentlemen all. And if that's any use to you, you're welcome to it, I'm sure.'

More beer had made him repetative, but not more informative.

After this disappointment, Jim had had to rely further on the assertions and conjectures of the Wickhams' fellow-students and contemporaries. They maintained that after a term or so of offering discreet daytime entertainment to various young sprigs of the aristocracy, Lucy had become disillusioned, perhaps because she had hoped to entrap one of these good friends into a more lasting arrangement. She had then changed her tactics, and had accommodated a series of dons, virtually all of them teachers of English, and all of them, presumably, in a position to further her husband's career. How far this was a successful move was not known for certain. However, it had been gradually mooted round the college and the literary clubs of the university that Wickham, far from being the intellectual booby that he had first been thought, was in fact one of the most promising brains of his year. The fact that this reputation was belied by appearances was not of any great importance, since such reputations almost invariably are belied by appearances at Oxford. Luckily all his tutorials were enjoyed alone with his various tutors, so there was little that his fellows could do in the way of checking up on the current gossip, even if they had been interested enough to do so. Most of them were simply after a quick degree, so they were not.

Certainly his conversation did not betray his hidden genius, though several fellow-students, now mostly sunk into alcoholism and schoolmastering, remembered a memorable night when he had got stinking drunk at the Lamb and Flag, had talked about what his wife was currently engaged in with a Fellow of St John's, had gone into considerable detail about that gentleman's sexual tastes and practises (which had nothing to do with swans) and had been arrested by the Martyrs' Memorial, telling it kindly that he was not allowed home until eleven-thirty. A brief newspaper report of his appearance in court was appended in photo-copy.

But if there was method in Lucy's spare-time work, it apparently had not paid off. Perhaps the reason was that two of the examiners in the year of Wickham's finals were raging homosexuals who could not by any stretch of the imagination have laid themselves open to Lucy's blandishments. At any rate Wickham got a second, which some thought was better than he deserved, and speedily returned to that haven of Oxford seconds, his home land. He had tried to maintain his contacts for some time, but the dons and contemporaries to whom he wrote seemed to have stored his letters in out-of-the-way nooks or seldom-opened drawers, or perhaps they simply forgot who he was – at any rate they had not replied. Nothing at all had been heard of him in recent years.

At the end of his report, Timmins had to address himself to the relevance of all this to the murder of Professor Belville-Smith. He had to admit right away that as far as he could see, there was no connection between the two whatsoever. All the obvious possibilities had been checked. He could find no record of Wickham having gone to him for tutorials, and no record of tender friendships formed at Parson's Pleasure; nor had Belville-Smith been on the examining board when Wickham took his Finals. He had made diligent enquiries as to whether Belville-Smith and Lucy had been rumoured to have had any scandalous relationship, but he had been met with nothing but amused incredulity. 'My God, man,' said one of Belville-Smith's fellow dons, 'the old man must have got over that sort of thing round about nineteen-twelve.' Nor had anyone been able to take seriously the idea of Belville-Smith as the practiser of secret vices, a furtive visitor of ladies who did him unmentionable services. 'Everyone knows everyone else's business here,' said this same source, 'and as far as that kind of thing goes, Belville-Smith *had* no business.'

Bill Bascomb rummaged through the pile for more, but was disappointed. He was surprised to find that his glass was still full.

'No, not a bad headache,' said Alice O'Brien into the phone, automatically wrinkling her forehead to give verisimilitude, 'not a *really* bad one. I think I've just got a bit run down, what with this murder, and everything. I'll be all right . . .'

The Principal of Daisy Bates College had had a strong suspicion that Alice was wallowing in the murder, but she was a woman with a strong leaning towards pharmacology, one who at exam time turned herself into a travelling quack, haunting the corridors and curing and causing minor ailments. Alice knew that the way to her heart was through a trivial symptom, and she readily received permission to skip dinner, even though tonight was a guest night.

'I'll come and see you after they've gone,' promised the Principal. 'I've got some new pineapple-flavoured dispril I'd rather like to try out on you.'

Alice repressed her usual reply about throwing physic to the dogs, and uttered soft words of gratitude. Then she sat behind her study curtain waiting for her and Dr Porter's little flock to get their gowns on and go up the hill towards Hall. It took longer than usual, since on guest nights there was a chance that one of the young lecturers, either presentable or eligible (they were seldom both), might spot one of them through the crowded room, and look on them with the eye of passion. So as they went in a giggling gaggle up the hill, their gowns were thrown back around the armpits, to reveal figures in various stages of over-development. Alice sat behind her curtain, noting the occasional face:
'Janelle Whyte – clumsy child . . . Ruthie Martin . . . that little bitch Dodds . . . Jaynie Taylor (wipe that silly smirk off your face, for God's sake) . . . Prue

Parsons . . . Soo Wong, or is it Woo Song? . . . Pippy Warren . . .'

When she got to twelve, the college was at last still, and she breathed a sigh of relief. All Dr Porter's flock were gone to dinner. She felt purposefully in her hair, and pulled out a hairpin.

The Porter lived a couple of corridors away. Alice had to resist the impulse to slink or skulk, knowing that this invariably resulted in the members of her moral tutorial group being caught when they tried their hand at shop-lifting. So she marched in Dr Porter's direction with a brow so furrowed that anyone could have guessed that her purpose was to borrow an asprin. There was not a cockroach stirring as she went along, but when she came to the door she gave a regulation sharp tap on it – the sort of knock that intimates to any watcher that the knocker knows that the occupant is not there, but is doing it for form's sake. Then she inserted her hairpin in the lock after the briefest of looks around, and disguised it as best she could with the key to her own door. Alice had a strong wrist. It was miraculously easy. In a matter of seconds she was walking confidently in, shutting the door, and looking around in the half-light of the early evening.

She had, she thought without surprise, not been in Dr Porter's room since the early days of the latter's fellowship at Daisy Bates – days when a few feeble attempts had been made at an all-girls-together atmosphere. They had speedily found they had nothing whatsoever in common beyond their sex and their department, and had dropped anything more than distant courtesy (and frequently that too). Her first impression of the room was that it was fantastically, disgustingly tidy. It was the most unlived-in room she had ever known. All the cushions on the sofa had been plumped up, all the curtains fell in neat parallel folds, the mat had been placed four-square in the middle of the room. She had not expected dirty undies, but this was going too far.

She moved over to the desk. Pens and pencils of various kinds and colours were ranged in parallel lines on a desk-set of very good plastic. There was a neat hole for an inkwell, a square for rubbers, and grooves for plenty of writing implements. In the centre of the desk was a blotter, but the usual obligingness of blotters in the matter of yielding clues when read backwards was missing here – it was hardly marked. Alice shook her head at the unacademic tidiness of it all, and made a tentative pull at the drawers down either side of the desk. Writing paper, typing paper, paper tissues, exercises from external students, internal essays spattered with various marks of disapproval ('wild generalization', 'hardly vouched for by the facts' and so on) – and then one drawer that was locked, on the bottom right-hand side. Such a challege was not to be resisted. Alice immediately sank to her knees, and dived for another hairpin. A little reluctantly the lock gave way to her twistings.

It was not quite the conflagration she had been banking on. At the top of a little pile was a booklet called *Simple Sex-Talks for Girls*, issued by the Church of Scotland Moral Welfare Committee; two large colour photographs of Donny Osmond and one of a pop group so physically repulsive that one might have guessed they were sponsored by the Pope were the next exhibits; under them was a pulp magazine, very old, entitled *The Eighteen Loves of Lana Turner* (the true story told by a friend); lastly came a copy of *Song of the Red Ruby*, and underneath that, a carefully folded pull-out from a magazine. Gingerly removing and opening it, Alice found it to be a well known art-work, featuring Burt Reynolds, apparently without clothing.

As she meticulously put each piece back in its place, she speculated distastefully on the personal meaning of this little collection. Could it be that the repulsive Beatrice actually drooled over cut-outs of Burt Reynolds in the privacy of her own study? Could she have crushes on pop groups, an intense curiosity about the private lives of faded film stars? Reluctantly she decided that this could not be the case. Could it be, then, that she was so infected by the general atmosphere of girls' boarding school which afflicted the college that she confiscated, actually confiscated anything regarded as likely to corrupt the little dears' rural simplicity? Reluctantly she decided that it could. She felt that the Church of Scotland Welfare Committee would be surprised to find itself classed as objectionable, along with Agnar Mykle and Burt Reynolds. She considered they ought to feel flattered.

Bill Bascomb was interrupted in the reading of his Oxford dossier by a call to exercise his powers as a moral tutor. There seemed to be a party in the block, and as he had not been given the statutory ten days' notice in triplicate, he felt the need to go and investigate. There was always a danger that the affair would be reported to the Master by one of the students from the Evangelical Union. As he might have guessed, the party was an impromptu one given by a crowd of enormous rural science students, one of whom had just received an alcoholic tuck-box from the ancestral vine-yards. As the least of them was apparently three times his size, he swallowed his principles and volunteered to type a retrospective request for permission when he returned to his room. It was generally agreed that he was a good sport. He then accepted a couple of glasses of Australian whisky, did severe damage to his insides by actually drinking them, and left the party at the point where some of the bawdy songs – very rural, if not very scientific – were being repeated for the ninth time. He then poured himself a couple of quick sherries to take the taste of iron filings out of his mouth, and settled down to do justice to the dirt on Peter Day.

Peter's stay at Oxford had been comparatively short. He had apparently arrived there early in the summer of 1954, and had somehow managed to get a temporary job at the Bodleian Library. Luckily a young librarian who began there only a month or so later was now in a position of some influence in the library, and he remembered Day very well. Day had a degree from Leeds, and a letter of recommendation from the Head of the English Department there which seemed, with hindsight, to be cunningly ambiguous – one of those letters which doesn't stop you appointing someone, but allows the writer to imply that he had warned you if any disaster occurs later. Day had also done some tutoring for the Adult Education people in Sheffield and Leeds, and some of his stories from that period of his life were still remembered:

'Indeed, I could tell you them word for word,' his old co-worker, now deputy chief cataloguer, had said, 'because I heard them so often, as did everyone who worked here at the time. I very much doubt their veracity. I've been to Sheffield.'

He had claimed to be engaged in a research project centred on Victorian theatrical adaptations of Dickens novels, and had even done a bit of unearthing – several dreadful travesties of *Oliver Twist* and some ridiculous continuations of *Edwin Drood*. This had all been done in his first summer. However, soon after that he settled down to a life of pub-crawling with the undergraduates, who apparently accepted him as one of themselves. He very soon had a regular circle of cronies in most of the well-known hostelries. The cataloguer had come across many who believed he was a member of their own college. In the course of the next year he had changed his research topic several times, and usually hit on some unfathomable topic on which he was unlikely to meet with anyone who would insist on engaging him in troublesome conversation – subjects like the later novels of Fanny Burney, of the dramas of Bulwer-Lytton. Nothing was known to have come of these studies. Very little, indeed, emerged from his professional activities as a cataloguer, and it was a great relief to his superior (who had a rather squeamish distaste for his post-alcoholic breath and the stale tobacco aroma sticking to his clothes) when he was on one and the same day found to have been sleeping for the past month in a very large drawer in one of the cellars, using a medieval illuminated manuscript as a head-rest, and also accused by one of the young lady librarians of attacking her sexually in the middle of the eleventh century. This last accusation was disbelieved, since accusations of this sort are made by all librarians every three or four months, but it had proved a happy excuse for giving him the sack.

Peter Day had been very genial about it. He said he was grateful to them, because he was beginning to think he was vegetating. He had picked up his nylon shirt and his toilet bag (also concealed in one of the drawers in the cellar) and had gone off. He had dropped hints that he would probably next try Canada, where he said he had contacts – which probably meant old drinking cronies.

All in all, it was a tract for the times. It might have been sketched by Kingsley Amis before he started to like Mozart. Equally, it was very much what Bill Bascomb would have guessed without the aid of Jim Timmins's research. The rub was that, as with Wickham, there was not the slightest connection with Professor Belville-Smith. The deputy head cataloguer had great difficulty identifying the latter, who had certainly never been in the library in his time to his knowledge, but he knew of no contact whatsoever between Day and the regular academic community. He was quite sure he had never had any official tuition or supervision – 'what was there to supervise', as he said? Nor was Belville-Smith, as far as Timmins could gather, likely to frequent any of the places where Day was in the habit of spending his lunch-times and evenings. Belville-Smith ate in Hall, and drank in his rooms. He had checked on possible links with Wickham, but of course he and Lucy had departed to make names for themselves in their own country some years before Day staggered up to Oxford.

Summing up, Timmins had to confess that he had drawn a blank. But to maintain his sense of superiority – he was from Balliol – he did allow himself a rather smug remark about what extraordinary people seemed to manage to get academic appointments in the colonies, or did one call them dominions now?

Alice felt a little better when she got into Dr Porter's bedroom. The air of academic sterility in the study had been over-powering – the sort of atmosphere that made you wonder what you were doing with your own life. And each of the Fellows' flats had a door from there bedrooms leading to a Fire-escape, thus ensuring an easy exit for the Fellows and such girls as desired in the event of a mass invasion from the men's colleges. If the Porter was heard to come into her sitting-room, a quick escape was possible, if not very dignified.

Beatrice Porter's bedroom was, like her study, a model of neatness and propriety. There was nothing to suggest to the most fevered imagination that this bed had actually been slept in by a human body. Alice peered short-sightedly into the wardrobe, but was too intimidated to rummage as she had intended, for Dr Porter's ineffably boring Sunday School clothes were hung up in a neat row, brushed, mothless, colourless, sexless, immaculate. The least touch, it seemed, would infect and leave traces. Alice peered down at the shoes, which were similarly innocent of the knowledge of human feet, and gave up in despair. The chest of drawers which she next tried contained what might be described as a good class of underwear, all neatly stacked in piles, all looking in what a philatelist would describe as 'mint condition'. As she stood back and surveyed the room, the fantasy came upon her that Dr Porter did not exist. Perhaps this room was assembled to give credibility to a double identity, perhaps Beatrice Porter was in reality Australia's Mata Hari, who spent her nights seducing secrets from the inscrutable Chinese diplomats in Canberra. Or perhaps she was a fantasy in the collective minds of the English Department, and someone had given surface credibility to the fantasy by assembling a collection of utterly anonymous clothes and shoes, and pens and rubbers, so that all that was lacking was a face and body. Then she thought of Dr Porter's face, and the whole idea collapsed.

In a frenzy prompted by the notion that Dr Porter might slip away early from coffee with the guests, which she was inclined to do if the discussion turned on anything other than the further restriction of visiting hours, she went from bedside cupboard to toilet cabinet, she poked the immaculate bed (and had great trouble in unpoking it), put her head under it in search of trunks – trunks full of antiquated contraceptive devices, trunks full of secret, privately-printed books on Mark Akenside from which had been cut and pasted snippets which had together made up the Porter thesis. Even boxes of cheap brandy, tins of cream cakes, even a packet of dates would be welcome. Some proof of hidden fires, hidden desires, the vaguest inclination towards – not vice necessarily, but inviduality.

It was not to be. As Alice O'Brien slipped down the fire-escape into the gathering gloom, Dr Porter still remained in her imagination, upright, characterless, non-existent, a monument to Australian wowserism, the achieved non-person. My God, thought Alice, she's going to go far.

The level of Bill's sherry flagon had slipped down to danger level, presaging drought and a bus-trip to town ('town', thought Bill drowsily in inverted commas) for a refill next day. Australian sherry was certainly something you could get used to, he thought, if you gave it a chance. They ought to make more of it in the Australian House hand-outs, those treasuries of seductive fantasies. He poured himself another, and looked at the last page of Jim Timmins's report:

'Can find no trace of a P.R. Doncaster at St Catherine's in 1939. There is a C.R. Doncaster in 1942. Is he the one? Am beginning a preliminary investigation.' Bill pulled his mind up. Doncaster – had he heard a Christian name? No, he didn't think so. Must be a misprint, either in the college record or in the prospectus of the Drummondale School. Probably the latter. But Royle had said '39. Doesn't matter a monkey's fart, he thought blearily. He dragged himself to his desk, pulled out his typewriter, and started typing tomorrow's lecture on *The Phoenix and the Turtle*.

CHAPTER SEVENTEEN

Party-Spirit

Menzies College was in festive mood. Most of the chairs had been cleared out of the senior common room, and in the kitchens little bits of New Zealand cheddar were being attached to little bits of sweet gherkin by means of sticks – toothpicks from Norway, which made the occasion truly international – and then left to dry out in the afternoon sun. In addition, flagons of lethal red wine and still more lethal sherry stood in a shady alcove at the back of the common room, young lady Fellows from Daisy Bates College and Dame Patty College had been invited (once their names had got past the censorious scrutiny of the Master), and the student leaders of each block had not only been invited along but had been allowed to bring their steadies, though in return for the dry cheese and dry conversation they were expected to act as waiters for much of the evening.

It was a wine and cheese party, and little else had been talked about in the corridors of power for the past week. It was, after all, the first party since the Belville-Smith murder, and though no one could think of any reason why this one should have a bloody aftermath, well – the Belville-Smith murder had been pretty irrational anyway, as far as anyone could judge, so it was just possible that this one might too. Certainly they all hoped so. A bloody aftermath was infinitely better than the hangover of accusations and recriminations which was the usual aftermath of most of the parties in Drummondale. Thus, there was, for this occasion, a quite unusual preponderance of grateful acceptances over regretful refusals.

On the guest list there was, in addition to the Fellows and moral tutors of the various colleges (young lecturers who still found that the convenience of free meals outweighed the disadvantages of the awfulness of them), the governing body of the college – Professor Wickham, Mr Doncaster, and a few other choice souls who were slaving to make Menzies College an Oxonian oasis in the midst of savagery; there were also the heads of the other colleges, and a few isolated graziers. The Principal of Daisy Bates came with a reticule of pills and potions for sicknesses caused by excessive indulgence. The graziers were mostly from the older or wealthier families in the district, men who were expected (wrongly) to be favourably disposed towards the college and likely to leave a sizeable bequest to it in their wills. Among these were the Turbervilles; the Lullhams and the McKays were not thought to be sufficiently big fry. So enough of the merry gathering at the Wickhams' were there to cause a rather pleasant frisson to run through those who had not been invited on the previous occasion, a frisson which was increased by the arrival of Miss Tambly, whose presence no one could account for, unless the Master had been doing a bit of amateur sleuthing on the side and was trying to recreate the circumstances of the Belville-Smith murder.

As usual the affair had taken a little time to warm up (though the sherry was already unpleasantly warm). Everyone got into incongruous little groups, and found it difficult to get out of them. The Master of Menzies

College had the knack of dogmatism, and his pronouncements sent rippling waves of silence in his wake. Nor was social savoirfaire conspicuous among the rest of the guests. Miss Tambly sailed in like one of those new American aircraft carriers designed apparently to hold the entire US Navy, and boomed across to the Master:

'Nice of you to ask me. Quite a surprise. Pleasant little set-up you've got here. Scruffy but serviceable. Reminds me of my war days – same sort of cheerful make-do.'

The Master hardly accepted this as the high praise the speaker intended, and gruffly gestured towards the flagons. Miss Tambly abruptly changed course, shaking hands around as she sailed, and causing all those who had ever before felt the imprint of her massive paw to shrink into the shadows. Having equipped herself with a large tumbler of red wine, she found herself by Merv Raines, and they sank into conversation – her part consisting of barking, his of grunting.

'Now as suspects go,' said Bill Bascomb, in his jolly, tactful manner, standing in the middle of the floor talking to Alice O'Brien and a handful of students, 'she'd be the one I'd go for, everything else being equal. She's got the muscle, and she'd have the nerve, and say what you like it must have taken a lot of nerve.'

'Don't see that,' said one of the students. 'He didn't look as if he had much fight in him. In fact, I'd back almost any of you against that old bird.'

'So would I,' said Bill. 'Though I don't like the "of you". But what about hopping in the window, what about putting on your plastic overalls, or mac, or whatever it was, to make sure you didn't get bloodstains on you? Would you fancy skulking in that waste lot on a fine night in a plastic mac, and squeezing through that window.'

'Not much of a squeeze,' said Alice. 'It was a perfectly

good size window, and it wasn't very far off the ground.'

'I realize you're the expert on breaking and entering,' said Bill, 'but I'm talking of the purely psychological problems.'

'Anyway, since the old bird was half-asleep when he gave his lecture,' said the student, 'he was probably out like a light as soon as his head hit the pillow.'

'You can say what you like,' said Bill, 'but I'd need plenty of this inside me' – and he held up his glass of red wine.

'You *had* plenty of that inside, remember?' remarked Alice.

The topic could not be got away from in the other little groups scattered all around the common room.

'How did the school take the murder?' said Bobby Wickham genially to Mr Doncaster. 'Bound to appeal to a boy's mind, I suppose. Is it still the main topic of conversation there?'

'God, my husband is a bore,' said Lucy to one of Bobby's Honours students. 'You'd think we'd had enough of the murder by now, wouldn't you?'

'They can't get enough of it,' said Doncaster. 'They were bitterly disappointed when I wasn't arrested the next day. Some of the younger ones apparently hoped I'd be hanged on the spot in the quadrangle. They're running a book, I believe, and I gather I and Miss Tambly are neck and neck at the moment.'

'Great wishful thinkers, the young,' said Bobby.

'My feeling is,' said Lucy, turning round, and unable to resist what was in fact still her favourite topic of conversation, 'that he must be a very unintelligent murderer. After all, if he had only stuffed a pillow over his mouth for a couple of minutes, then put it back under him, it would probably have been put down to natural causes, and we wouldn't have had any of this nastiness.'

'You're surely not suggesting,' said Doncaster, looking a little startled, 'that you'd *like* the idea of living in this little town knowing there was a murderer at large?'

'My point is that I *wouldn't* know,' said Lucy. 'In any case, I *do* know there is a rapist, a wife-beater, a man who sleeps with his own daughter and seven or eight rampant practising queers within a square mile of where we live, so I don't see that the odd murderer would make a great deal of difference one way or the other.'

Lucy at an academic function was rather different from Lucy among the graziers, but the difference, as someone had remarked, was only between her being unintentionally embarrassing and being intentionally embarrassing. On the whole the latter mood was to be preferred.

'What's your own particular little vice?' she said, turning back to give her attention to the student.

'Political situation's a bit confusing,' said Merv Raines, expanding conversationally in his relief at escaping at last from the clutches of Miss Tambly.

'Is it?' said Bill.

'The question is, what Whitlam is up to,' said Merv.

'I always find Australian politics confusing,' said Bill, 'so I wouldn't notice the difference.'

'What's so bloody confusing about them?' asked Merv, aggressively and illogically.

'Well, I still haven't worked out the difference between a premier and a prime minister,' said Bill.

'Christ, you bloody Pommies,' said Merv, unconsciously stepping up the Australian content in his accent: 'you're still living in the colonial age, the lot of you. You'd like to send out some bloody chinless wonder from the Royal Family to be Governor-General, like in the old times.'

'We can't,' said Bill. 'The army needs all the men it can get at the moment.'

'You'd like to rule us from Whitehall,' said Merv, who could never forgive Britain for giving Australia independence without making her struggle for it, 'you'd like some snotty little civil servant to make all our decisions for us, ruling the savages for our own good.'

'We've got enough savages to rule in Northern Ireland, thank you,' said Bill. 'We're not taking on any more at the moment.'

'You bloody toffs from Oxford,' said Merv, his voice becoming more and more like a disagreeable Indian stringed instrument, 'you've never done a hand's turn in your lives, put your shoes outside your door at night, leave the washing-up for the servant to do, call your man to fetch your buttered scones from the JCR . . .'

'I always got my own teas,' said Bill. He glanced over to where Mr Doncaster was gracefully handing Dr Porter a glass of lemon squash, and made off in their direction. He was in no mood for a great Australian punch-up. Merv looked highly deprived by his departure, and seemed to be looking around for another Englishman.

'Very confusing, the political situation,' said Mrs Turberville, to a lanky student who was feeding her with cheese-filled footballs, 'very confusing indeed.'

'Too right,' said the student.

'I've always said,' said Mrs Turberville, raising her considerable voice as if she were addressing a public meeting, 'that this fellow Whitlam ought to be tried for treason, and then put against a wall and shot.'

'Oh, I don't know,' said the student tolerantly.

'The trouble with the university,' said Mrs Turberville, 'is that it's red, through and through, infiltrated by Peking . . .'

* * *

'Of course, Augustan satire is quite beyond the average student's comprehension,' said Dr Porter to Mr Doncaster and Alice O'Brien.

'Certainly we don't find much in the way of subtlety among our boys,' said Mr Doncaster, seeking desperately with that furtive wandering of the eyes people who are cornered at parties get for some means of escape from Dr Porter's idea of party small-talk.

'Take the Modest Proposal, for example,' said Dr Porter.

'I beg your pardon,' said Mr Doncaster.

'Relax,' said Alice; 'she's not making you an offer.'

Mr Doncaster smiled vaguely, as if this was witty conversation at a level in which he could not hope to participate, and turned with relief as Bill Bascomb approached in flight from Merv Raines.

'Very confusing, the political situation,' he said.

'I've just had that one,' said Bill. 'Do you think we could try the drought for a change?'

But he looked very preoccupied, and he was. He paid little attention to the attempts at conversation. A word was buzzing around at the back of his mind . . . half-formed . . . tantalizing . . . screaming to come out . . . a word . . . something he had been reminded of . . . a word . . . a memory.

'Let me fill your glass,' said Mr Doncaster in desperation to Alice.

'Have you tried the new toffee-flavoured laxatives on your girls?' said the Principal of Daisy Bates College to Miss Tambly. 'I've had some very interesting results from them.'

'Don't believe in all this coddling,' said Miss Tambly brusquely. 'Toffee-flavoured, my fat aunt. If medicine's going to do any good, it's got to be damned unpleasant. We give cod-liver oil for most things. Tried and tested. If we didn't do that, we'd have them round the dispensary the whole time. The governors are very down on that sort of expenditure, you know. Never make a profit that way.'

'How difficult for you to have to think of things like that,' said the Principal, with genuine sympathy.

Miss Tambly was just about to say something very Australian about institutions which were supported by tax-payers' money when they were interrupted.

'What ho!' said a voice from the door. 'A festive scene, eh? Hospitality? Conviviality?'

'Christ,' said Alice in her least sound-of-music voice, 'who invited you?'

'No one,' said Dr Day, steadying himself against the back of an armchair, 'but I am not insulted. I am willing to subscribe to a polite fiction that the invitation was lost in the post. Provided, of course . . . provided that now I have smelt you all out, you keep me well filled for the rest of the evening.'

'I wonder,' said Lucy Wickham, gazing through the thick air towards the ceiling, 'why we have to be embarrassed everywhere we go by the behaviour of Bobby's staff.'

'Lucy, old fruit,' said Dr Day, making an alcoholic lunge in her direction, 'long time no see. I hear you've been getting friendly with the police force, is that right? I suppose that's why you've been neglecting your old friends.'

At a sign from the Master, who had thus far in the evening fulfilled his hostly duties by keeping to a dark corner and emitting waves of taciturnity and discomfort, the student waiter-guests left their various positions and clumsily guided Dr Day to the drinks alcove, where they surrounded his swaying form and shielded the sensibilities of delicately-nurtured Australian females from the shock of his bleary appearance.

'The English department does it again,' said Alice cheerily to Mr Turberville.

'That chappie seems to have a drink problem,' said Turberville, surprisingly quick on the uptake.

'His only problem is how to get enough,' said Alice.

'You look as if you had a headache coming on,' said the Principal of Daisy Bates College kindly to Bill Bascomb. 'I have some very good tablets here, that you can actually dissolve in whatever you're drinking, and it removes the nastier effects.'

'Seems a pity to ruin good grog, doesn't it?' said Bill. 'Anyway, it's not a headache.'

'Some personal problems, I suppose,' said the Principal. 'I can understand that. It's so difficult for you young men, just out from England. Torn between two civilizations . . .'

'Two?' said Bill, passing his glass through the phalanx of students' bodies around Dr Day, and receiving a full one in exchange. 'But it's not a personal problem either. I'm too young to have personal problems. It's just a word . . .'

'A word?'

'A word I'm looking for. It's buzzing around my head. It came to me earlier in the evening, then it went away, and I can't get it back. It's quite an ordinary word, I remember that.'

'I didn't know you were *creative*?' said the Principal, with an odd mixture of admiration and disapproval.

The evening ended as these evenings almost always did. The drinks ran out rather earlier than usual, and it was generally agreed that it had not been a good idea to closet Dr Day and five healthy, thirsty students together around the drinks table. Still, there wasn't much acrimony on this score, because most members of the party were fairly satisfied with the high number of suspects that had been assembled to appease their appetite for sensation. Some had even got a mild frisson out of conversing with one or other of them; it was, in fact, the first time Dr Porter's conversation had ever caused a frisson. Most of the suspects saw quite enough of each other in the general course of events to be happy at a fairly early termination to the evening, especially as most of them had been sufficiently 'in' to get an adequate supply of the lethal red liquid; and the number of empty flagons piled up under the table testified that no one had positively gone without. So they drove off into the night in straggling groups: bumpers were dented, jovial curses were uttered, cats were slaughtered on the roads home. Gradually a sort of peace descended on Menzies College, except around one far block, from which a country and western record in praise of the Vietnam war could be heard through an open window.

The fresh air hit Bill Bascomb hard. He had been conversing for some time with the Principal of Daisy Bates, and had convinced her that he was a very nice boy, possibly going to the bad, but still very pleasant and understanding. His head was also filled with sherry, and filled with a word. A word that would not form itself into letters or into sounds. A word that was a mere notion, a shade, an ambiguity. He staggered along in the waste land between the five blocks, confusedly looking round and wondering where he was and which block was his own. The music did not lessen the confusion in his mind. 'What We're Fighting For', a paean in praise of napalm, juggled around in his head, and he stood clutching a crude wire fence, and hazily imitating the imagined gesture of the singer. That boy is all soul, he said to himself. He saw a tree, and made for it, seeing it as a stable centre in a shifting world. A shifting, spinning, tipping, crumbling world. The white blocks all around him danced, changed positions; some of the stars in the sky zoomed towards him, and then zoomed away again. Suddenly, as he clutched the trunk for safety, the word came to him, from nowhere, from the sky, put itself in his mind, and exploded there, adding sparks to the dancing, shifting stars.

'That's it,' said Bill loudly. 'I bet that's it.'

Then his legs gave way, and he sank to sleep around the roots of the college gum-tree.

CHAPTER EIGHTEEN

In At The Kill

'But I've got it,' said Bascomb, late next morning, sitting in the arm-chair of his office at the department and looking scruffy and dishevelled. 'I've got it.'

'You quite patently have *not* got it,' pointed out Alice O'Brien, 'since you've forgotten it again.'

'It came to me,' said Bill, drumming his fingers distractedly on the arms of the chair. 'Just before I conked out, it came to me suddenly – I knew that was it.'

'Are you sure it wasn't just some drunken dream or other? I wouldn't mind betting it was that. You've been thinking pretty hard about this — for you. I expect it all got into your dreams, and you just think you got the answer.'

'It wasn't a dream at all, I tell you. If I can just get on to Timmins to check for me, it will solve the whole thing. Just one word . . .'

'Obviously a dream,' said Alice, who never gave up. 'The word will suddenly come back to you, and it will be something absolutely useless like "cucumber sandwiches" or something.'

'It was not a dream, and it did mean something,' said Bill with dignity. 'But it certainly will come back — I'm sure of that.'

'Oh God; so we're going to have you going round agonizing over that blasted word for the next few weeks, are we?' said Alice. 'If I were you, I'd forget it entirely – then if there really is anything in it, it will come back when you least expect it.'

'I've got plenty else to think about, heaven knows,' said Bill. 'The Master sent me a note this morning asking me to explain how come I was found curled up around a tree by one of the domestic staff.'

'*Pas devant les domestiques* is very much his code,' said Alice. 'Well, good luck with your explanations. If you could only bring yourself to salute and call him sir you'd be all right. Still, I can't imagine you'd break your heart at getting the push, would you?'

'Well, no,' said Bill, 'not as far as the company is concerned. But it's all that cooking I shouldn't like if I set up on my own. You'll have to invite me to all the guest-nights you can. Do you think I could get a season-ticket?'

'Possibly. The Principal did say at breakfast that you were a well-conducted young man. But she looked suspicious when I burst out laughing, and anyway she's probably heard already about your love-affair with the gum tree. She doesn't like anything out of the ordinary.'

Left to himself Bill groaned, and put his face in his hands. It was tormenting – to have had the word and forgotten it. And it is the clue to the whole damned business. This way madness lies, he thought. He resolved to follow Alice's advice and try to put the matter out of his mind altogether. He grabbed a book from his case willy-nilly, opened it, and began to read:

And as in some cases of drunkeness, and in others of animal magnetism, there are two states of consciousness which never clash, but each of which pursues its separate course as though it were continuous instead of broken (thus, if I hide my watch

194

when I am drunk, I must be drunk before I can remember where), so . . .

'I must be drunk before I can remember where . . .' Bill let the book rest on his knees, then turned over to look at the title. It was *Edwin Drood*.

'Bloody good advice, Charlie boy,' he said.

The saloon bar of Beecher's Hotel was aswill with beer, and so was Bill Bascomb. He was at that stage where one begins not to notice one's surroundings, which was just as well, for no Australian saloon bar at six-thirty in the evening really bears noticing. One can count oneself lucky if one can get one's feet out of the spreading puddles of beer on the floor. Bill had finally found himself an uncomfortably high stool, and he sat there looking red and dyspeptic. He belched very loudly every ten minutes or so in the approved manner, and the other drinkers around thought that he might be, in spite of appearances, a very nice type of chap. There was a little party of station hands beside him, with wide hats and long limbs, and high brown boots which allowed them to scorn the swirling puddles beneath them. When Bill drained his glass and ordered his third schooner, one of them said to him kindly;

'A yew English, or somethin?'

'I'm afraid so,' said Bill.

'No need terpoligize,' said the man generously. 'Takes all sorts, arfterawl.'

' 'Sright,' said his mate.

'Ya like Strylian beer?' said the first, in the condescending manner of a Florentine asking a visitor if he admired the 'David'.

'Yes, very much,' said Bill, who knew which side his bread was buttered. 'It's just the bubbles I can't get used to.'

The conversation lapsed for a few mintues while his new friends pondered whether he had intended to insult the Australian nation as a whole. Luckily they decided he was just ignorant.

'Yer werkear, do yer?' asked the first, turning to him again.

'Yes, I'm up at the university,' said Bill.

That explained it. It was just ignorance.

'Nice set-up yerve got there,' said the man.

'Yes, real nice,' said Bill, who had been long enough in the country to know all the conversational ploys.

'Some pretty funny characters, though,' said the man.

'Too right,' said Bill, from his heart.

'Some real drongos,' said the man.

'Yeah, some real no-hopers,' said Bill.

'Yeah, some real ning-nongs,' said the man. Bill hoped this wasn't some sort of competition. But his friend managed to hop out of the groove he was lugubriously ploughing:

'Not that they're all English, by any means,' he said, bringing out his new thought expansively.

'No, that's true,' said Bill.

'Lotter them er New Zealanders,' said the man.

'Yes, New Zealanders are the worst,' said Bill.

'Yer couldby right,' said the man. 'There's a right lotter drongos comes from New Zealand.'

'Yeah, a lot of no-hopers,' said Bill, who knew his cue by now.

'Wa wud yew say, Charlie,' said the man, turning to his mate, who was gazing pensively into his brown, bubbly glass. 'Would yer say New Zealand or Britain produced the biggest load of ning-nongs, taking it by and large?'

'Oh, New Zealand,' said the second station-hand. 'Not a doubt of it. Now, yer meet some real nice Englishmen, once in a while.'

'That's true,' said the first, including Bill in the compliment. 'A real nice type, setches yerself.'

'Much obliged,' said Bill.

'Then there's that other pommie,' said the second man. 'The one that usually comes in here around four o'clock. Yew know, that one from the Uni.'

'Harf the bloody Uni's in here at four a bloody clock,' said the first man, after pondering a while. 'Which one do yer mean, Charlie?'

'That one who's always half-pissed before he arrives, Dave,' said the other. 'You remember, told us all about Oxford, some libry eruther. And about some place called Sheffield, or something . . .'

'Oh, you mean Peter Day,' said Bill Bascomb.

'That's it,' said Charlie. 'Peter Day. Bloke innis fifties. That's the one. Yer know him then?'

'I should do. He's a colleague of mine,' said Bill, thinking this was one place where he didn't have to feel ashamed of the fact.

'Well, I'd say he was a real good sport,' said Charlie.

'Yes, a real good scout,' said Dave.

'A real good cobber,' said Charlie.

'One of the best,' said Dave meditatively. 'Here, where are yer going then?'

They gazed at the fast-retreating form of Bill Bascomb, who had pushed open the swing doors into the foyer and fallen head first over the fringes of the tattered carpet.

'Must be gointerbe sick,' said Charlie. ''E lookeda bit greener bout the gills.'

'All these bloody pommies do,' said Dave.

But in their insular prejudice they did Bill Bascomb an injustice. As they spoke, he was already half-way to the emergency telegraph office of the Post Office, a few yards down the main street.

Inspector Royle had had a rather up and down time since the night of the rain making (which had not produced rain). The next two days had been spent in bed, recovering from the unaccustomed exercise, and

197

grunting at intervals with pain and bad temper. What he was mainly worried about, apart from the possibility that his morning dates would be looking round for more reliable partners, was the ridicule which he anticipated from the rest of his loyal team when he returned to the station. However, he had obviated that by the simple device of telling them nothing about the events of that evening at all. He calculated rightly that not one of them would have turned up at the right spot, so that if they didn't hear the details from him, they wouldn't hear them from anyone. Thus, he maintained an enigmatic silence, broken only by mysterious hints of secret knowledge, and all his underlings said among themselves that Royle was a deep one, and no mistake.

Now he was sitting bolt upright in his desk chair, very inspectorial, and furrowing his brow. He was also groaning inwardly. He hadn't had to think so hard since he had been on the track of the mysterious graziers' conspiracy, and since the failure of that little piece of detection (failure so far as the murder investigation went, that is, for he had some thoughts of making a good thing out of it, banking on the local graziers' hatred of appearing ridiculous) he had not held thinking in particularly high esteem.

'I just can't get what you're getting at,' he said wearily. 'Let's start again at the beginning. Cut out the smart-aleck stuff and give it to me straight. And you'd better make it convincing, because he is one of our most respected figures.'

'Not for long he won't be,' said Bill confidently. 'Look, from 1938 until 1941 he was a scout at Jesus College, Oxford. That's what this telegram from my mate on the *Oxford Mail* means.'

'Fine body of boys,' said Royle, in an apparently

198

automatic response. 'I can't for the life of me to see what that's got to do with murder.'

'A scout,' said Bill slowly, 'is a college servant. That's why the damned word kept buzzing around in my brain — every time I saw him handing someone drinks, it started again. A scout is a man who cleans out the students' rooms, washes up for them, fetches their meals — *waits on* them, if they can afford to pay him. That chap was a trained waiter, and you could see it in his whole body.'

'So what?' said Royle. 'A man can't help it if he hasn't had your chances. This is a democratic country. You've got a down on him because he's not one of the top bracket. You aristocrats!'

Bascomb's parents came from Dulwich, but this didn't seem the time to bandy around family trees.

'He was a scout at the college until 1941,' he said, 'and then he went into the army. Do you get it now? And he came to Australia as soon as the war ended, in 1946.'

'Well, so bloody what?' said Royle exasperated. Is it a crime not to have had much of an education? Why even I myself . . .'

'You don't put MA Oxon after your name,' said Bill. 'Eh?'

'You don't claim to have a degree from Oxford.'

'Well I've never heard him claim that either, come to that,' said Royle. 'Who says he claims it?'

'We established right at the beginning that the prospectus of the Drummondale School says he has an MA from Oxford. Obviously they got their information from him. At any rate, they can hardly have got it from Oxford. He always says he went to St Catherine's, which hasn't got any college buildings, so no one knows anyone else there. If anyone else came along who was there at the same time, he wouldn't necessarily be exposed.'

Royle took some time to digest this.

'So, what you're saying is that he's claiming a degree, and he hasn't a right to it — is that it?'

'You've got it in one,' said Bill.

'Well, now, even you would admit that something like that is hardly a matter for the police, surely?'

'It is if he kills someone to keep his secret,' said Bill.

'Now, you've got no cause to say that. Where's your proof? I ought to warn you that Mr Doncaster has some very powerful friends in this town. What evidence have you he killed the old bugger?'

'Firstly, he's the only one with a shadow of a motive, right?'

'You don't get a conviction on motive alone, you know. You can't go along to a judge and say "this man had a motive — convict him" ' (though God knows he had done just that often enough — and got his conviction at that). 'You've got to have other things — bodies and weapons, and things,' he concluded lamely.

'He had the opportunity as well. You've got no check on his movements after he left the Wickhams'.'

'Nor on anyone else's except yours,' said Royle, keeping his end up well.

'But the vital clue is the conversation at the Wickhams'. It's there he'd break down. All I'm asking is for you to go along and question him again, and then bring this casually up, just in the middle of the conversation, and watch his reaction.'

'You're joking. All hell would break loose if it was wrong.'

'It's not wrong. Don't you see, it all hangs together. Let's go over the whole thing. Doncaster is a scout at Oxford, just before the war, and in the first months. We have definite proof of this from Timmins. He's a bright boy, but there aren't many chances for a bright boy in the thirties. While he's there, he keeps his eyes open, gets the manner off pat, gets the accent, gets the walk

– everything. Now Belville-Smith is a don at another college, but they've never seen each other as far as Doncaster knows. He's a pretty dim figure in Oxford life in any case, so he wouldn't make any impression on his memory. At any rate, when he turns up here as a visiting Professor, and Doncaster is invited to the Wickhams' party, he doesn't think for a moment that there is anything to fear from him. Simply doesn't give it a thought. He's met plenty of Oxford people in his time in Australia, and no one has thought to question his claims.'

'How come he gets to be a headmaster in Australia?' asked Royle. 'You can't just walk into a job like that.'

'Well, not quite, but very nearly,' said Bill. 'He comes out with the early migrants after the war. Applies for a job in a private school. Claims an Oxford degree. Nobody checks up. It's as easy as pie. Nobody's ever checked up on my degree, and I'm at a University. Those private schools are so hard up for competent staff that they practically beg people to fool them. And with a manner like that, he probably had them queueing for his services.'

'Then no one checked up afterwards either? I can't believe that. He's been in schools all over the country – real good schools at that. He had a couple of terms at Geelong.' He pronounced it as if it were Valhalla or Ninevah.

'But once he was in, he was in. Nobody was going to check up after that. He had excellent references from his previous school, and that was that. And frankly, you don't need much knowledge to get by in most of these schools, so you can be pretty sure the references were always good. Then along came old Belville-Smith, he was invited to meet him, and he was so sure of himself that he went along.'

'And you think Belville-Smith recognized him?'

'Well, I shouldn't think he did anything as positive as

that in fact, as far as I could see, it could be that he didn't make any connections at all. You remember what happened: the conversation turned to scouting, and the poor old bugger's state of mind being what it was, he sort of "went off", and kept on repeating the word over and over again. He was pretty squiffy by then, remember, though nobody was quite sure how much was drink and how much was natural. Perhaps there was a little bell rang in the back of his mind – sometimes it does with very old people. But I wouldn't mind betting there was nothing in it at all: he was just vaguely repeating things. I noticed he did it once or twice when he was talking to me, just saying the word over. He wasn't focussing, couldn't concentrate properly. But obviously Doncaster didn't take it like that – you can see how it affected him.'

'You think he just upped and murdered him.'

'Yes. Panic reaction. But on the whole he hadn't very much to fear. Firstly, there was nothing on the surface to connect them; then the obvious people whom the police were likely to investigate most thoroughly were all in the English department, people who'd been in contact with him for some days and had studied in his own field.' He wanted to add 'and then, he knew what the Drummondale police were like', but he thought better of it.

Royle sat there for a minute, slowly thinking.

'Well, it could be. I'll give you that,' he said. 'There'd be plenty of knives and what-not around in the rural science labs at the school. I've been around and seen 'em.'

'And a bloody lab coat wouldn't cause any particular comment,' said Bill.

'No. They do some pretty nasty experiments there, some of those little buggers,' said Royle, with envy.

'Exactly. Easy as falling off a log.'

'Yeah . . . But as far as asking me to go to him with a lot of conjecture like that — well. I just couldn't do it. It'd be more than my job's worth, you must see that.'

'I thought your future depended on finding the murderer?' said Bill.

'On finding *a* murderer,' said Royle. 'It might be different if he wasn't the head — just a teacher, or someone at the high school. But then again, he's on the executive of the Country Party. If I went to my superiors with a story like you've concocted about a chap like that, one of the big shots around here, well, they'd practically clap me in my own cells. If you're going to arrest a chap in his position, you need three or four actual witnesses — all of them ministers of religion at that.'

'I'm not suggesting you consult your superiors. Just you go and have it out with him.'

'Alone? Are you off your rocker? Look, mate, I'm a married man. I've got two daughters at home — depending on me.' (Royle did this line very badly indeed.) 'Course, I'm as brave as the next man — especially when the next man is you —' he gave a coarse laugh — 'but I'm not going to go to his study and practically present my throat to him and say, "Have a slice if you feel like it, old man".'

Bill was getting more and more desperate. What is more, he rather resented the crude slur on his courage, which was as great as the next man's, especially when the next man was Royle.

'Look, if you're not game, I'll do it. *Provided*,' he put in hastily, '*provided* you're willing to have me watched day and night after I've done it. You'll need to have two or three men in the college grounds, and I want your best men at that. The next time there's a party, or when it's non-resident Fellows' night at Menzies College, I'll bring up the subject of scouts. I'll make it pretty clear to him that I know his background. I guarantee it'll drive him off his rocker, and that's how we'll get him.'

But they never did fix the murder of Professor Belville-Smith on to Mr Doncaster in a court of law. It was for the murder of Bill Bascomb that he was caught and sentenced later in the year.

Bestselling Crime

☐ No One Rides Free	Larry Beinhart	£2.95
☐ Alice in La La Land	Robert Campbell	£2.99
☐ In La La Land We Trust	Robert Campbell	£2.99
☐ Suspects	William J Caunitz	£2.95
☐ So Small a Carnival	John William Corrington	
	Joyce H Corrington	£2.99
☐ Saratoga Longshot	Stephen Dobyns	£2.99
☐ Blood on the Moon	James Ellroy	£2.99
☐ Roses Are Dead	Loren D. Estleman	£2.50
☐ The Body in the Billiard Room	HRF Keating	£2.50
☐ Bertie and the Tin Man	Peter Lovesey	£2.50
☐ Rough Cider	Peter Lovesey	£2.50
☐ Shake Hands For Ever	Ruth Rendell	£2.99
☐ Talking to Strange Men	Ruth Rendell	£2.99
☐ The Tree of Hands	Ruth Rendell	£2.99
☐ Wexford: An Omnibus	Ruth Rendell	£6.99
☐ Speak for the Dead	Margaret Yorke	£2.99

Prices and other details are liable to change

ARROW BOOKS, BOOKSERVICE BY POST, PO BOX 29, DOUGLAS, ISLE OF MAN, BRITISH ISLES

NAME...

ADDRESS...

....

....

Please enclose a cheque or postal order made out to Arrow Books Ltd. for the amount due and allow the following for postage and packing.

U.K. CUSTOMERS: Please allow 22p per book to a maximum of £3.00.

B.F.P.O. & EIRE: Please allow 22p per book to a maximum of £3.00.

OVERSEAS CUSTOMERS: Please allow 22p per book.

Whilst every effort is made to keep prices low it is sometimes necessary to increase cover prices at short notice. Arrow Books reserve the right to show new retail prices on covers which may differ from those previously advertised in the text or elsewhere.

Bestselling Thriller/Suspense

☐ Skydancer	Geoffrey Archer	£3.50
☐ Hooligan	Colin Dunne	£2.99
☐ See Charlie Run	Brian Freemantle	£2.99
☐ Hell is Always Today	Jack Higgins	£2.50
☐ The Proteus Operation	James P Hogan	£3.50
☐ Winter Palace	Dennis Jones	£3.50
☐ Dragonfire	Andrew Kaplan	£2.99
☐ The Hour of the Lily	John Kruse	£3.50
☐ Fletch, Too	Geoffrey McDonald	£2.50
☐ Brought in Dead	Harry Patterson	£2.50
☐ The Albatross Run	Douglas Scott	£2.99

Prices and other details are liable to change

ARROW BOOKS, BOOKSERVICE BY POST, PO BOX 29, DOUGLAS, ISLE OF MAN, BRITISH ISLES

NAME...

ADDRESS ....

....

....

Please enclose a cheque or postal order made out to Arrow Books Ltd. for the amount due and allow the following for postage and packing.

U.K. CUSTOMERS: Please allow 22p per book to a maximum of £3.00.

B.F.P.O. & EIRE: Please allow 22p per book to a maximum of £3.00.

OVERSEAS CUSTOMERS: Please allow 22p per book.

Whilst every effort is made to keep prices low it is sometimes necessary to increase cover prices at short notice. Arrow Books reserve the right to show new retail prices on covers which may differ from those previously advertised in the text or elsewhere.